BACKWATER BAY

A KURT HUNTER MYSTERY

STEVEN BECKER

THE WHITE MARLIN PRESS

————

Join my mailing list
and get a free copy of my starter library:
First Bite

Click the image or download here: http://eepurl.com/-obDj

For those that like to follow along or are interested in the location of some of the key scenes in the book please go to:

https://stevenbeckerauthor.com/locations-in-my-books/
Here you can find interactive Google Maps

The Kurt Hunter Series

1

STEVEN BECKER

A KURT HUNTER MYSTERY

BACKWATER BAY

IF I'D HAD a knife I could have sliced the humid air like a loaf of bread; it was a day when I would rather have been somewhere else. Whatever parts of my body weren't covered by my wet, sticky uniform were coated with fiberglass dust. It was misery at its finest, and I longed for the crisp air and cold streams of the Sierra Nevada. The locals said if you lived in South Florida long enough you became acclimatized. Since I'm from Northern California, it took some getting used to. It'd been a month, and I didn't think I would ever be comfortable here.

The entire neighborhood was out watching, playing, and helping me repair the Park Service boat that I had run into the dock last week. Adams Key wasn't much of a community, but the small island with two houses was my home. By Caesar Creek, the popular pass to the Atlantic Ocean from Biscayne Bay, the small atoll sat in the middle of Biscayne National Park. Ray was helping me—or rather, I was helping him—repair the damage I had done to the bow last week when I misjudged the wind and current and came in too hot on the concrete dock. His wife, Becky, was sitting under a palm tree watching their son, Jamie. Zero was doing what Zero does—barking at everything that moved.

This kind of repair was new to me, and watching Ray work, I wasn't sure it was something I would ever be good at. I was more a wanderer than a workman, which was a good fit for my job— patrolling the national parks. While Ray laid up the fiberglass and resin over the foot-long scrape and we waited for the chemicals to cure, I watched the parade of boats stream by, on their way to the ocean side of the barrier islands. Then it was my job to sand. Through three different grits, I shaped the resin to match the contour of the boat. Feathering the edges was a little tricky, but with Ray's guidance, I was getting the hang of it.

"You think this is the last coat?" I asked.

"Maybe one more. We can lay it up tonight, then sand and paint in the morning."

"Cool. I gotta work tomorrow. Do you have time early?"

"Dude, I got nothing but time. Martinez can be as pesky as those No-See-Ums with y'all agents, but I'm a lowly maintenance guy. He looks at me like I'm one of the greenskeepers at those fancy golf courses he's always talking about. Unless there's a brown spot on the putting green or such, we're invisible."

Ray had pretty much summed up my boss. From my short experience with Martinez, I had learned he liked things clean, simple, and off his desk. Ray's job was to maintain the buildings and infrastructure of the park. Something, after a decade here, he could do on autopilot. For an area with a permanent population of a dozen—the four and a half of us here and two other families on Elliott Key—he was the man. From the lighthouse up on Boca Chita Key to the two campgrounds in the park, he kept the outer islands working. He was a happy man, but Becky was getting anxious about bringing up their two-year-old son, Jamie, a twenty-minute boat ride away from the closest street.

"Why don't you finish that up? I'm gonna grab a shower, another beer, and fire up the grill. We can cook up some of them fresh tails me and Zero got this morning," he said. Grabbing his tools and supplies, he walked toward the small shed by his house.

I had heard about the underwater exploits of the pit bull mix with the eye patch that reminded me of the Little Rascals' dog, Petey.

Becky picked up Jamie and turned to me. "Hey, Kurt, how's about you keep an eye on old Zero for a few? Got to get the young'un down for a nap and get a little quality time with the old man."

That was a little more information than I needed, but she had one of those singsong Southern accents that you couldn't say no to. Not that I would. Zero was about all I had for family here. Just when the first sign of the fiberglass mat started to show through the smoky resin, I stopped sanding and cleaned up the rest of the supplies. Taking a few steps back, I looked at the boat, still not satisfied it would pass muster under Martinez's critical eye. He was far more interested in the condition of the equipment and facilities than in doing investigative work. It was all by the numbers with him. Hopefully, the final coat of resin and paint would blend it all together.

I was halfway down the path to my house when I heard the whine of an outboard engine. A bird's-eye view of my neighborhood would clearly have shown the deepwater channel called Caesar Creek. Named after Black Caesar, the famed eighteenth-century pirate who plied those waters, the winding channel was the only pass from the bay to the Atlantic for miles. From my brief explorations of the small keys, shoals, and lagoons, it was no wonder that pirates and smugglers had used this area to hide out. It was a complicated maze of mangrove islands, lagoons, creeks, and shoals.

If I wanted to fill out incident reports all day, which would have made Martinez a happy man and my life easier, I only had to stand on the long concrete pier outside my front door. Although it was a well-marked pass, many boaters, either lacking in patience or not paying attention, misread the shallow waters and grounded. I'd usually check that they were okay and leave them in the hands of Sea Tow or BoatUS. There were ordinances about damaging the fragile seagrass beds, but most of the groundings were accidental.

It was the sound of the engine that was bothering me. Even my inexperienced ear could tell from the high pitch that the driver was running too fast. Approaching from the ocean side, the go-fast boat sped by the dock, rocking my Park Service center-console and causing me to hold my breath hoping the fenders would protect our repairs. These were the guys who made my job hard. Besides their other nefarious activities, they liked to flex their horsepower and often pushed other boaters out of the channel and into the shallows. Looking to the left, I saw the boat fly past Caesar's Rock. Instead of following the main marked channel into Biscayne Bay, the boat turned hard to port, cutting around the piling with the square green 23 placard attached to it.

After a month there, I knew the main cuts and passes, but there were areas I hadn't yet explored and this was one. I was still green as a boater and had taken to using the kayak I had found leaning against the house to both explore some of the sketchier areas and get some exercise. From studying the charts, I knew the deepwater channel the boat had entered passed between Rubicon and Reid Keys. It was unmarked and ended in an area called Islandia, which, although it sounded exotic, was pretty much a swamp with winding creeks connecting the bay and ocean. These were smuggler's waters. The eye of Hurricane Andrew had passed directly over this spot in 1992, cleaning out the old buildings and shacks, but the trade remained.

Nothing good went on in these backwaters. I ran to the dock and jumped down to my twenty-two-foot center-console. In less than a minute I had cast off the lines and was under way. Expecting trouble, I pulled my webbed gun belt from the console and, steering with one hand, put on the belt and checked the weapon. The gun did little to calm my nerves as I stared at the screen of the chart plotter watching the depth drop from ten feet to three in seconds. The cut suddenly ended and I slipped into neutral. With delusions of building some great resort, developers had dredged channels like this one in the fifties and sixties. They were abandoned now, marked yet still dangerous. The boat coasted to a stop and I looked around. I didn't need the electronics to know I was surrounded by shallow water. The brown color all around me was a sure sign that I should exercise caution.

I dropped the Power-Pole to anchor the boat and cut off the engine. It was quiet now. Waiting for the last of my wake to wash through the mangroves, I listened for any man-made sounds. The outgoing tide pushed against the hull, but the pole held and I waited. The usual sounds of birds squawking and fish jumping were gone. It was too quiet. Looking around, I zoomed the chart plotter in on the area, trying to figure out where a boat that size could be.

The guidebooks showed the famed Florida Keys extending from Key Largo, at the southern boundary of Biscayne National Park, a hundred twenty miles to Key West. Geologically, the chain of islands began fifteen miles above Key Largo and ended seventy miles past Key West. Biscayne National Park was a unique environment, billed as 95 percent water. There was a lot of blue out there but also a lot of shoreline. Most of this was mangroves, which trapped everything the tide brought in—and from my short time there, I knew most of it was trouble.

A small boat-shaped icon showed my position, and I scanned the display in search of an adjacent area I knew. For the past month, I had been methodically exploring the park. Starting at Bayfront Park on the mainland in Homestead, where the headquarters building was located, I had worked my way south along the shoreline, which was crosshatched by the grid of cooling canals for the Turkey Point nuclear plant; through Card Pass to the Card Sound Bridge; and back via the chain of barrier islands.

If the blue water and brown land were reversed, it would have looked like the Plumas National Forest, where I had been stationed before I was relocated here. The forest had a network of trails and fire roads that resembled the channels and passes here. Much like the huge expanse of water in Biscayne National Park, not much happened on the vast land tracts that made up the forest. It was the thin lines on the maps—streams in the forest and islands in the park—that attracted man.

In the national forest, I had soon found the best way to walk my beat was by working the streams. And the best way to work the streams was by fishing them. It had taken time to learn to read the water out west, but once I did, it allowed me to discover the largest pot grow ever found on public land.

If I hadn't been fishing, I never would have noticed the small current running through an eddy. It looked unnatural and I followed the flow, uncovering the intake for an irrigation line that ran up the steep banks and serviced the grow. That find had gotten me publicity I didn't want, which had split my family and now had me in the Park Service version of the Witness Protection Program. It may have ruined my life, but it hadn't made me quit fishing.

Fly fishing had become a passion and I relished the opportunities the bay offered. After hooking a small tarpon on a spinning reel when I first got there, I was addicted. Fishing fresh and salt water were different and I still had a lot to learn. Practicing my casting on moving water taught me not only the secrets of the bonefish, tarpon, and trout but also showed the cuts and eddies I would never have noticed just cruising by.

The quiet was broken by an engine starting. My right hand instinctively went to my gun, and I waited. Instead of coming toward me, the sound receded. The boat was moving away. I looked down at the chart plotter, zoomed it in as far as it would go, and saw the small channel labeled Hurricane Creek that I guessed the boat had escaped through. The engine noise soon faded entirely as the boat moved on and I was stuck staring at the shallows off Totten and Old Rhodes Keys. I was unfamiliar with the water there, so this was as far as I would venture in the Park Service boat. Martinez might have gotten over the scrape, but a tow bill would put him over the edge.

With my prey gone, I pressed the button to raise the Power-Pole. I waited for the current to move me into the channel and saw several fish jumping at the entrance to a small creek on Rubicon Key. Curious, I idled closer to the inlet and watched the water. The tide was moving quickly, making it easy to see the main channel, and I inched forward. Several more splashes caught my attention. The depth finder read eight feet and was holding steady, giving me a little reassurance as I entered the creek.

There were no soundings on the chart plotter, so I was running mainly on instinct. The depth finder was helpful, but one of the first lessons I had learned was that the transducer, being mounted on the stern, showed where you had been already and not where you were going. Still, it was reassuring to see the depth remain constant. Watching the color of the water for any sudden changes that would indicate shallow bottom, I moved into the interior of the key. Fish continued to jump around me and I lowered the Power-Pole, reached around into the console, and pulled out my fly rod.

After assembling the eight-weight, nine-foot rod, I installed the reel and fed the line through the eyelets. I tied on a twelve-foot leader, then looked at my fly box and chose a Clouser Minnow. The yellow and white streamer with two eyes didn't look like it would fool anything, but once it was in the water, fish went for it. Without knowing what species I was casting for, this was my go-to fly. Stripping a dozen feet of line off the reel, I moved to the open bow and started with a few false casts before allowing the fly to drop on the water. Once it did, a swirl came up behind it, and with my heart beating hard, I used my left hand to strip in a few inches, raising the tip of the rod with each pull to make the fly swim. It only took two pulls before the fish took the fly and ran for the mangroves. The rod bent under the strain, and with the line pinched between my left index finger and thumb, I gauged the stress on the line.

If I'd been in open water, I would have allowed the line to slide between my fingers until the slack was taken up and I could fight the fish on the reel, but the fish was heading hard for the mangroves. With the line held tightly between my fingers, the rod was almost bent double as I reeled in the slack, and I finally breathed when I could release my left hand and fight it on the reel. Now, with the leverage afforded by the rod and drag on the reel, I pulled the fish away from the roots and worked it toward the boat.

I saw a brilliant silver flash and then the black lateral line that told me the fish was a snook—my first. But the fish had other ideas after seeing the boat and doubled its efforts. Even assisting the drag by cupping my hand on the reel to slow the line, there was no stopping the fish as it ran for the mangroves. I fought back, using the rod again to try to pull the snook to open water, but it was deep in the root system. I felt the line go slack and I knew the fight was over.

Fishing is an emotional roller coaster. The most thrilling feeling you can get is when the fish takes the bait or lure and the fight begins. The most defeating feeling is when the line goes slack and you know you've lost. It was the latter I was experiencing as I cursed under my breath and started to reel the line in. It came freely for about ten feet and then stopped. Already frustrated, I was about to give a hard tug to free it from the root or branch it was caught on, not really caring about breaking the line and losing the fly, when I felt it move.

2

STEVEN BECKER

A KURT HUNTER MYSTERY

BACKWATER BAY

I KNEW it wasn't a fish. There's some kind of instinctual feeling an experienced fisherman gets when he is connected to something alive. There are the telltale signs: the downward pull, the shake of the head, or the run. Whatever I had snagged was not alive.

Like most fishermen, I hated to lose gear, and although it was a two-dollar fly on the end of the line, I pressed the button to raise the Power-Pole and, with the boat free, began to pull. If you've ever held a baby, you know the difference between dead weight and live weight. Without the stress of a fish on the end, the eight-weight line was strong enough to pull the boat toward the bushes. Fly line is pretty heavy-duty. Unlike mono or braid, PVC-coated braided Dacron is rated based on the weight in grains of the first thirty feet. The actual breaking strength of the bright yellow line was probably nearly thirty pounds.

I was close to the snag when the T-top of the boat brushed against the outer branches of a mangrove, forcing me to change tactics. Setting the Power-Pole again to anchor the boat, I pulled the line hand over hand until I saw the clear monofilament leader. I had to be careful now. The entire stress was on the dozen feet of twenty-pound test. Slowly I retrieved the line until I saw a dark shape emerge from the mangroves. At first, I thought it was organic matter, a mass of branches and mud. That proved not to be the case when I saw the neoprene covering and knew I had hooked a body.

Everything changed now. I was on the clock and there were procedures to follow. Reluctantly, I took out my cell phone and called Martinez. Half a dozen rings later, I breathed a sigh of relief when the call went to voicemail. As professionally as I could, I described the find, being careful to give the date, time, and location. With that out of the way, I scrolled through my contacts and called the Miami-Dade medical examiner's office.

The Park Service shared resources with both Miami-Dade and the Florida Department of Law Enforcement. Although I preferred working with the FDLE, the lab and morgue in South Florida were run by Miami-Dade.

I heard Sid's nasal New Jersey whine after the second ring and I relaxed. Even after only a brief acquaintance we were on a first-name basis. It didn't hurt that we shared a friendship with Justine from the crime lab. Sid was something of a father figure and mentor to her. At the moment, I wasn't sure what he thought of me. I did get the feeling that he liked me, maybe because I had suffered through the better part of an autopsy of another floater without losing my lunch. I imagined him staring over his reading glasses as he hunched above his desk, leaning too close to his pad of paper as he wrote down the particulars.

I gave him the GPS numbers, which served as an address out on the water. The satellite system, originally dedicated to the military, was public now and could pin down a location anywhere on the planet within about thirty feet. Water was as much a part of South Florida law enforcement as land. When Sid said he'd be there in an hour, he knew what was involved.

With the Power-Pole holding the boat in place and nothing to do but wait, I clipped off the end of the leader and set the rod aside. From a small box in the console, I pulled out another section of fluorocarbon and tied it to the line. There were only two flies left. I chose the chartreuse-and-white pattern and tied that to the end of the leader. Glancing over at the body, just to check that it was still there, I moved to the bow and started casting into the current.

I wasn't expecting much, just trying to kill some time, when the first bite came. A few minutes later, I had a keeper-sized mangrove snapper aboard for dinner. Two more followed, and I had almost forgotten about the body when I heard the whine of a motor approach.

The sound stopped just about where the deepwater channel ended, and I heard a call for the Park Service come through the speakers on the VHF radio. Per Park Service protocol, I was monitoring channel 16. After I answered, we switched to channel 17 and I was able to guide the sheriff's boat into the small channel.

I cringed when Sid saw the rod. Before I could offer an explanation, he called over.

"That it there?" he asked, pointing to the black lump in the water.

"Yeah, pulled it out and left it as soon as I saw what it was," I said. With Sid, at least, I wasn't too concerned about the circumstances that had led to my finding the body. Even Martinez would probably become so sidetracked by the paperwork required for finding a dead body in the park that he'd forget to ask. I pointed to the floater with the rod tip, surprised how quickly I had become acclimated to death. A month ago, when I'd first arrived there, I would have spent the time staring in morbid fascination at the body; now I fished.

He leaned over the gunwale of the sheriff's boat and said something to the deputy that I couldn't hear. The deputy walked around the center console, opened the hatch, and pulled out two sets of waders. Both men suited up, and I took their cue to slide into my own. I grabbed the waterproof camera and measuring tape, then checked my pocket to make sure I had a pad and pencil, something I had forgotten the last time we danced with a dead body in waist-deep water. We all looked at each other and eased into the water. The deputy reached over the gunwale and pulled down a red backboard.

I was right behind Sid, close enough that he swatted at me as if I were a mosquito as he started to examine the body. The last time we had been in this situation, I had been a virgin. Since then, I had learned my lesson, and after snapping a dozen or so pictures, I got out the pad and started to take notes. The deputy was doing the same and we had an awkward standoff when Sid was ready to roll the body.

With an eye on each other, we both put our pads back in our pockets and moved toward the corpse. There had not been much to see when it was facedown, just a body covered by a wetsuit. We all turned away simultaneously when we got our first look at the anterior.

Sid was the first to recover, and I snuck a look at the deputy, taking our unspoken feud to the next level by facing the body before he did. Almost immediately, I wished I hadn't and had to choke down the bile in the back of my throat. After several deep breaths, I had recovered enough to start recording what lay in front of me.

By the length of the hair, I guessed it was a woman, but from the crab-eaten face, I couldn't be sure. "They get the eyes and lips first," I said like I was some kind of authority. In fact, I was repeating exactly what Sid had said after we recovered the body of an anonymous Cuban refugee on the mainland side of the park a few weeks ago. He let the comment go and started speaking.

"Looks like a propeller got her," he said.

I took my eyes off what had been her face and looked down at the huge gash where her stomach had been. The wetsuit had been slashed open and an empty cavity showed where the stomach and other internal organs had once lived.

I was behind the curve now and took several quick pictures before pulling out the notepad and pen. "How do you know it was a propeller?" I asked.

Sid looked over his glasses and I could see the deputy grinning behind him. Score one for the opposition. I thought he was going to ignore me, but with a pencil, he pointed at the perimeter of the wound. "The water did us a favor in cleaning the wounds. The gashes are regular like the blades of a propeller. Around a thousand RPMs would be my guess. Anything faster would have shredded her."

I wasn't about to embarrass myself by asking how he knew this. I could figure out the math later. "Looks like a diving accident then?" I asked, confident that I had nailed it.

Before Sid spoke, I saw the look on the deputy's face and added another point for him. Two to one. "We're a long way from the cause of death. I would've thought there'd be some gear if that was the case," he said, giving me that look again.

The deputy was showing teeth now. If I could just get him to laugh, I could recover a point. "Right. Mind if I sit in on the autopsy?"

"I guess that'd be okay. You held your lunch last time."

In fact it had been dinner, and I had left before he started the internal examination. He hadn't yet made the diagonal incisions in the man's chest and removed the internal organs. That body had been in the water for only a few days. This one appeared to have been in for much longer. There was no bloating or gases. I figured this was due to the empty space where the woman's stomach should have been, but I wasn't in a position to voice my opinions. I was too far·behind to lose another point. Three points down would be too hard to come back from.

"There's nothing else here for me," Sid said.

As if on cue, the deputy pulled the backboard to the woman's side and together we rolled the corpse on and strapped it down. He moved first, pulling the body behind him, and I followed. When we reached the boat, he climbed aboard, and I helped push the body over the gunwale. Once aboard our respective boats, we pulled off our waders, and with the deputy in the lead, I followed them across the bay and into Government Cut. Shadows cast by Miami's skyline gave us some shade as we coasted up to the dock on Dodge Island.

Fortunately, the tide was slack, and with a light southeasterly breeze, I was able to execute an acceptable docking maneuver and keep the score two to one. I did forget to put the fenders out before docking, but the huge tires used to cushion the large freighters that often docked here worked for my boat as well. After tying off, and adding a spring line to keep the boat from being pushed forward when the tide started going out, I walked over to the deputy's boat and helped him load the backboard into the medical examiner's van.

We said a guarded goodbye and I went to the passenger side. Sid crawled into the driver's seat. I climbed in and buckled my seat belt then grabbed for any handhold I could find, knowing what was coming. He looked almost cartoonish. Sitting too close to the dashboard, with his head above the wheel, Sid pulled out of the parking lot, jumping the curb with the rear wheels as he turned onto the road, and ignoring the three cars that he had cut off as they honked and cursed. The rest of the ride was more of the same, and shaken, I climbed out of the van when we reached his office.

"Guard the body while I get some help," he said, climbing down from the van. As he walked to the entrance, I went around to the back doors. I was going to check that the body was all right after the wild ride there but decided that was stupid, almost giving the deputy that third point even though he was absent. Instead, I pulled out my phone.

"Justine Doeszinski," she answered after the receptionist routed my call to the crime lab.

"Hey, it's me."

"Hey, Me," she answered.

I totally deserved that and decided to counter with the one line that would work with her. "Got another body," I said.

3

STEVEN BECKER

A KURT HUNTER MYSTERY

"DON'T you dare start without me. I'm on my way," Justine said.

So what do you do when you suspect the woman you're interested in gets more excited over dead bodies than live ones? You take her to an autopsy, and that's exactly what I did for our third date. I wasn't sure if it counted as a real date or not, but I had called and asked her and she had said yes. Some women would react the same way if you offered up a Jimmy Buffett concert: Justine liked her work.

After waiting for two attendants to take the body, I headed into the building and nodded to the security guard. Although I dislike wearing a uniform, it does have benefits. I'd been here once before and knew the way. After descending the stairs, I followed the starkly lit corridor to the morgue, wondering whether fluorescent fixtures were mandatory in subterranean spaces. Inside the first room, I saw Sid through the glass partition and knocked. He came to the door and I told him Justine was on her way. This brought a smile to his face, and I remembered the jealousy I'd felt the last time I was here.

There were a few easy conversation starters in South Florida.

The weather was usually at the top of the list. With no tropical storms threatening, we moved on to fishing. Sid called himself retired now but had once been an avid bluefish and striper fisherman in the Northeast. I knew that an invitation to fish the bay would result in the end of his retirement and put that one in my pocket for a future favor. We made it through the twenty minutes it took for Justine to drive from Doral to Miami.

"Hey. You didn't start, did you?" Justine called out as she entered.

Before I could answer, she came over and pecked my cheek. I felt the blood rise to my face, partially from the contact, but also from the surprise. The medical examiner's office is not exactly the place you expect that kind of thing. She wasted no time donning the required gown, mask, and safety glasses. I caught a glimmer in her eyes through the acrylic shield that showed how excited she was.

I followed her into the room and the three of us stood around the stainless steel table. Sid smiled at Justine and started the recorder. It was all business from here. The basic measurements and data were all noted. Although he wouldn't comment, the body looked to me like it had been in the water a long time. He bagged and tagged samples of the woman's hair and nails, carefully inspecting what was left of her hands in the process.

"No sign of a fight," he said, laying down the right hand.

"How could you tell after she was in the water for so long? There are no fingernails." I stated the obvious, worried he would sense that my education on forensics came from an in-depth study of *CSI: Miami*. I had binge-watched every episode in preparation for my assignment.

"No bruising," he noted without further explanation, and moved on to her toenails. After inspecting every exposed part of her body, he took pictures of her face and wounds, then asked for help to turn her over. In comparison to her front, with her decimated face and the gash across her stomach, her back was fairly benign.

Using a pair of surgical shears, Sid started to remove the wetsuit. Cutting in a straight line from her neck to her legs, he peeled away the neoprene and started to examine what was left of her skin. If you had told me what I would be looking at before I saw it, I would have been worried, but it was so clinical it didn't really faze me. First, all the blood had long since left her body, leaving the torso china white. It just didn't look like a person anymore.

We rolled her back over and Sid cut off the arms of the wetsuit. He removed the remaining pieces and placed them in a large clear evidence bag. With that off to the side, he continued by making the standard diagonal incisions across her chest. Devoid of blood, the cavities seemed sterile, and I was losing interest, watching Justine more than the autopsy. Unlike her, I liked live bodies. My mind started to drift to the other two live women in my life.

It had been months since I had seen or heard from my ex-wife, Janet, or our fourteen-year-old daughter, Allie. I had stirred up a hornet's nest by finding the pot grow, and a week before the trial was scheduled to start, our house was firebombed. It had been the last straw in a crumbling relationship, and the next day I found myself in a judge's chambers for an emergency custody hearing.

Maybe I should have fought harder, but Janet's attorney's argument made sense to me as well as the judge. If they hadn't gotten me this time, there would likely be a next. Both my family and I were in danger. I suspected they were in Orlando with Janet's sister but had no proof of that. Part of my decision to come to Miami had been the proximity to where I thought they were; the other was the lure of the water.

I'm reclusive by nature and had no problem living in a neighborhood of two houses on an island five miles from the mainland. It all sounds romantic, but in reality, even for me, it could be boring. Fishing got me through most of those times. As I looked at Justine, I wondered how this tendency of mine to seek the perimeter of civilization would affect our relationship. It was exactly this that had caused the rift between Janet and me. We both wanted to live in small towns; the only problem was our conflicting definitions of "small". The population sign on her idea of a small town had five figures; the one on mine had three.

A humph from Sid brought my attention back to the table. I saw the lung in his hands. He turned it sideways and inspected it, then placed it on a scale and recorded the weight.

"Lungs show signs of expansion," he said.

I let it pass, not wanting to interrupt, but started paying attention. The other lung was on the scale and with its weight recorded, I looked at what was left of the woman's face. Squinting, I tried to get a picture of what she had looked like and succeeded to some degree, although whether my fantasy matched reality, I had no idea. What I did see was a faint blemish on the side of her neck. Moving closer, I saw what I thought was the faintest outline of a tattoo.

"You see something?" Justine asked, coming beside me.

"Here." I pointed to the area on her neck.

"Hey, Sid, take a look at what Sunshine found."

The three of us stood together. "Looks like a bruise to me. The body is covered with them. After being chewed by the propeller, it would probably have been slammed by the hull; it's exactly what I would expect." He moved the overhead light. Looking at the surrounding areas, there were indeed light bruises all over the body.

I looked at things from different angles than Sid and Justine, who were methodically working their way through the autopsy protocol. It was my job to find out what had happened, and the first thing I needed to do was establish her identity. The mark on her neck was no help now that I knew it was a bruise, but there might be something else.

"Can we get dental records or fingerprints?" I spurted out, knowing I had crossed some kind of invisible boundary when they both stared at me. Leaving the body to the professionals, I picked up the plastic bag holding the pieces of the wetsuit and stared at the material.

It didn't take long for a green slime coat to grow on anything in the water, and the wetsuit was no exception. It looked to be a light-weight suit. For a minute I just stared at it, remembering the scene in my mind when I had pulled the body from the mangroves. Something wasn't right. It didn't take the towering anvil-shaped clouds or the thunder from the late-afternoon storms to remind me it was summer. I didn't need to be a Florida native to know that the wetsuit was overkill in these waters this time of the year.

I looked back over the autopsy table and saw Justine taking fingerprints from the permanently wrinkled fingers. I felt stupid for asking about the fingerprints earlier and now held my tongue for a minute before she caught me staring at her.

"Yes?"

"How do you tell how long the body has been in the water?"

"Now the detective is thinking," Sid answered, his heavy accent making the comment seem more sarcastic.

I wasn't sure if this was a promotion or not and didn't tell him my title was actually special agent. He probably didn't care. "It's just the need for a wetsuit. The water, even out on the reef, is in the eighties this time of year."

"It's hard to determine, but I'd say only a few weeks at the most. I've seen a lot of bodies pulled from these waters over the years. All I have is anecdotal data, but you know when they went missing and you know when they were found. There're more precise methods, like the life cycle of a fly, to determine how long a body on land has been dead. Unfortunately, the water erases everything."

Despite his vagueness, it was my first lead. "Can we examine the suit?"

Justine set aside the fingerprint materials and looked at the evidence bag. "What are you expecting to find?"

"I don't know. Right now, it's the only evidence we have."

She looked at Sid, who shrugged. "I can't call this anything other than an accidental death at this point. There are no signs of a struggle. It looks like a boating accident, and I have seen enough of them to know what they look like," he said.

"If that's what he's going to put down for the cause of death, I can help find her identity, but that's about all my boss will go for. We don't have the budget to be chasing down non-murder, murders." Justine shrugged.

I looked at the body, feeling there was something else going on. "Can you give me some time?"

"I have to list a cause of death, but without an identity, there's no certificate or official filing. As long as there's room in the morgue, I can hang on to the young lady as a Jane Doe for a few days."

"Thanks," I said.

"You might want to hurry though. With the weekend coming up, things start to get lively down here." He laughed at his own joke.

"What about the wetsuit?" I asked.

"Justine can take it," Sid said, ending the discussion.

4

STEVEN BECKER

A KURT HUNTER MYSTERY

BACKWATER
BAY

THE EMPTY FEELING I had when I left the morgue and walked outside deepened when I realized I had no vehicle. Justine came up beside me.

"And you need a ride?" she asked.

"Yeah. I rode over with Sid."

She laughed. "I've had that experience. If you want to hang out at the lab, I'll take you back when I get off."

That would allow me to check the missing person database and I almost blurted out how convenient that would be. Fortunately, a voice inside my head reminded me that I had blown our previous date by being all about work. "Awesome," I answered smartly.

It was close to midnight, and I realized I hadn't eaten since before finding the body that afternoon. In light of the autopsy, that had probably been a good thing. As I sat in the passenger seat of the Miami-Dade police SUV, my stomach started to grumble and I thought a post-autopsy snack might be in order.

"Have you eaten?" I asked.

"So is this like dinner and a movie but with a dead body?"

I liked her sense of humor. "Maybe. Any ideas?"

She turned at the next light and pulled into a Denny's. "Not a lot of choices this late."

"Suits me."

She parked and we entered the quiet restaurant. This time of night, after the dinner rush and before the bars closed, it was quiet, and we sat across from each other in a booth near the back. I looked over at her and smiled. "You look nice."

Her dirty-blond hair was in tightly braided pigtails that sat just below her neckline. She lifted the ends and bounced them. "All day at the hairdresser's to get this look."

We laughed together. It was definitely a post-first-date laugh, one that came easily to both of us. That made me happy, and I watched her over my menu as her eyes darted back and forth across the page. Twice she caught me looking, and finally, I dropped my gaze and studied the menu. We waited in an easy silence for the server to come over for our order. After midnight meant breakfast for me, and I ordered a Grand Slam. Her clock apparently ran differently than mine and she ordered a milkshake.

We sat there quietly. I didn't really know where to start. I'd been to her apartment and stayed the night—on her couch. I knew she liked the water; both paddleboarding and diving had come up in our previous meeting. Other than that, we were strangers. Work was our common bond, but I was reluctant to go there.

"Been out on your board lately?" I asked.

She nodded. "I try to get out every day. At least my hours are good for that. Have you ever—"

The server interrupted us with our food before she could finish. The answer was no. I had started to kayak, mostly for the exercise, because it got really boring running around a tiny island. My powerboating experience was also limited, as the recent ding on the Park Service boat proved. Walking streams in the national forest had been my comfort level and I still considered myself a junior boater. I'd never tested the waters off the Northern California coast. They were a whole lot different from Miami. With difficult access, an ever-lurking marine layer, and the Pacific swell, boaters generally had to be hardier there. Feeling the air-conditioning in the restaurant made me remember that August could be the coldest month of the year on the Norcal coast.

She sipped her milkshake through a straw and I looked up between bites to see her watching me eat. "What?" I asked.

"It's okay if we talk about work," she said.

I was relieved for the permission but still hesitated, hoping she was sincere. She must have sensed this.

"So, I find it strange that our Jane Doe was wearing a wetsuit in August."

I took another bite, set my fork down, and paused. "I was thinking the same thing. There was no dive equipment either."

"I thought about that too. I'm guessing the straps of the buoyancy compensator were cut by the prop when it slashed her belly."

I thought about that for a second. "I wonder if the gear is where I found the body?"

"Good idea. I'm not thinking the fingerprints are going to get us anywhere. The tips were badly eaten. They're partials at best. Sid said her teeth were pristine. There won't be much in the way of dental records either."

I took another bite and picked up the last piece of bacon. "I still owe you a boat ride. Maybe we could have a look?" I knew I was offering prematurely, especially after catching a lecture from Martinez about taking other people on government property. It had been our first fight.

"We can sneak out like high school."

She said it with a smile and I hoped I was forgiven. "That'd be a good idea. Martinez is not going to be happy about another dead body, especially so soon."

"That dude should be thanking you. He was all over the newspapers when you and Mac Travis saved those women and took down that dirty detective."

"*We* took down the dirty detective. I'd be dead without you," I said. It was the truth. She had smashed Dwayne in the head before he shot me. "I still think he's hiding something."

"Welcome to Miami, Sunshine. It's not a matter of whether you'll become corrupt—it's when."

Unfortunately, I was learning this was true too quickly. "Got any forensics double-talk I can run past him and make it sound official?"

She was quiet for a minute and I wasn't sure if she was mad about the comment or just thinking. I finished my plate and heard a loud slurp as she sucked the bottom of her glass clean. "Ready?" I asked, picking up the check from the corner of the table.

"Yep. Back to the grind," she said, looking at her phone. "I get off at two. How about a little night run out to that secret island of yours?"

That both excited and terrified me. The thought that she might want to be alone with me on my island brought a shiver up my spine. Thinking about navigating Government Cut and the waters of Biscayne Bay brought me down to earth. In the end, I did what every guy would do and said: "Heck yeah."

Back in her office, watching her work, it was difficult to be all business. Attempting to look somewhat professional, I asked if there was a computer that I could use. She set me up at a station in an empty cubicle. I sat there watching her for a few minutes as she put on her headphones and moved to the row of stainless steel tables with different pieces of lab equipment spaced out across them. I could hear the faint sound of Bob Marley, which told me how loud the music was, and her body started to sway to the beat while she set some material on slides and stared into the microscope.

Looking away, I focused on the computer screen. Justine had logged me in, and I wanted to take advantage of the time and try to establish Jane Doe's identity. It would be much easier to move on if the crab-eaten face had a name. The problem was, not knowing how long she had been in the water placed her disappearance in an open-ended date range with hundreds of others. It was mid-August now, and just to make the search easier, I entered the month of July for a date range. I knew I was excluding data and justified it by calling this the center target range. Fancy way to say I didn't know where to start.

Over a hundred names with small thumbnail pictures appeared on the screen. I knew she was a Caucasian woman, which took the number to fifty. Apparently women went missing more often than men. The number was still unmanageable. I noticed the pictures looked mostly like mug shots of nefarious characters. Being a trained professional, I studied each picture and eliminated the ones that didn't look like divers, well aware there was no scientific basis for what I was doing. That took the number to twenty.

Staring at the missing women, I tried to superimpose the face of the woman in the morgue onto theirs. Despite the destruction the crabs had done, the bone structure gave me enough to eliminate a few more. I was feeling really good with a group of ten when Justine came by and popped my bubble. She must have seen I was on Dade County's website.

"The water's all connected. I'd be checking Monroe and Broward Counties too."

She was right and an hour later, I had expanded and refined my search using the same criteria. After eliminating everyone I could, there were still a dozen women who I felt could have been a match for Jane Doe. I looked up and saw Justine behind me. Her lab coat and headphones were off.

"Ready?"

I had gone as far as I thought I could. "Let's do it."

———

"You worried about taking me out?" she asked, breaking the silence.

I looked up and saw the sign for 836. We were almost to the causeway and I realized I hadn't spoken in a while. "Sorry. Just thinking about those women in the pictures."

"Yeah, now you start wondering what each of their stories is."

"That and I'm pretty sure one of them is her. There are other ways to go missing. In most cases, if it were foul play, we'd be unlikely to find a body."

"Dude, you found it fishing in a swamp. So, we're back to the accidental death by propeller?" she asked.

"I don't have much else," I said. "That's our exit coming up."

We were at the MacArthur Causeway and she turned off and made a left. "There's the lung thing," she said, and must have seen the blank look on my face. "Sid said the lungs looked like they had exploded."

"I recall something like that," I said, trying to remember what he had actually said. "We can check the transcript tomorrow."

"He didn't say it exactly like that, but that's what he meant."

I felt better about missing it. "Keep going straight here." I pointed past the cruise ships to the south side of Dodge Island. Justine pulled up into a space by the dock and we got out. Something didn't look right and I ran to the boat. The bow was out of the water and I knelt to ease the pressure from the line that I had tied too tight. I knew it was an outgoing tide when I docked and should have left more slack. Looking around, I saw Justine above me. It was bad enough to have made the rookie mistake, but now she had seen it.

Fortunately, I had tied the line off correctly and after releasing the bight, I was able to use the leverage of the cleat to ease the boat back into the water. I exhaled and, hoping my relief wasn't too audible, looked at Justine. She was staring out at the black water, probably deciding whether she could trust my boating skills at night.

"We'll take it slow," I said. One of the first rules of boating I had learned was that if you were going to hit something, hit it slow.

"No worries," she said.

I was both relieved and concerned, thinking I didn't have many more chances before she gave me up for an idiot. "Welcome aboard," I said lamely.

The pier was built for larger vessels and with the tide out, we had to get on our butts and slide down to the boat. Once aboard, I started the engine, thankfully not forgetting to put the kill switch key in, a mistake I had made too frequently. The engine wouldn't start until I inserted the plastic spacer. Together, we released the lines and the boat floated freely. The boating gods must have been watching me because with an offshore breeze and a slack tide we floated into the channel. I pressed the throttle gently, and the boat idled forward.

I kept the speed down and with the help of the chart plotter we cleared the last marker and were soon in open water. The route from there was anything but easy, but the electronics were my friend, and although my boating skills were just south of bad, I wasn't technically challenged. Marine electronics were much easier to navigate by than the hand-held GPS I had used in the backcountry. Glancing up occasionally to check for other boats or obstructions, I steered by the screen, following the colors and contours until we were in open water. My confidence was building and I nudged the lever forward until we were up on plane. It was exhilarating, running at night, and I looked over at Justine to see her smiling.

5

STEVEN BECKER
A KURT HUNTER MYSTERY
BACKWATER BAY

BISCAYNE BAY WAS NOT without its hazards. The shoals and obstructions were well marked during daylight hours, but few were lit at night. With only a sliver of a crescent moon, the water was ink black, barely showing the reflection of the channel markers. I had learned the bay, but even with the chart plotter to guide me, I felt safer in the deeper water on the outside of the barrier islands. The wind was down and we had a smooth ride past the lights of Key Biscayne. It was dark for a while and we could barely make out the fuzzy line of the Ragged Keys to starboard, but then the lighthouse on Boca Chita Key put me back on familiar ground. The landmark light was just visible over the low landmass.

Sands and Elliott Keys followed and I slowed, looking for the flashing red light that marked the entrance to Caesar Creek. Seeing it ahead, I steered to seaward, wanting to line up the boat for a straight shot at the channel and not ground trying to cut the corner like I had seen so many do. Once I was past the light, I handed Justine a spotlight and at just over idle speed entered the Caesar Creek channel that led to Adams Key. She panned the light across the water, catching the red and green markers that guided us home.

I had made it through the cut and saw the lights mounted to the concrete dock of Adams Key. My relief was short-lived—it was time to dock. With no wind, I just had to deal with the current, which, with the outgoing tide, would push the boat away from the dock. I'd done this before and knew if I took my time, I could get it right. Stopping in the channel about fifty feet out, I tied on the fenders to the port-side cleats. I breathed deeply and steered past the dock, turned around, and came back into the current. This would allow me to use the motor to place the bow where I wanted it. Coming in with the current pushing behind me would have been more difficult. Boats have no brakes, only reverse, which I had yet to master.

Easing the throttle, I nosed the bow to a piling with a cleat at its base and called to Justine to grab the line and tie us off. You can tell when someone has done this before, and it was apparent she had, which made me feel even more incompetent. Once the line was tied to the cleat, I dropped the engine into neutral and gently pulled the throttle back to reverse, allowing the engine to pull us back.

"Well done," she said.

I was tying the stern line and had my back to her, which was a good thing. If she had seen my childish grin at such a meager accomplishment, her estimation of me would surely have been lowered. Adding a spring line, I double-checked the ropes and stepped up to the dock. Before I could offer her a quick tour, I heard a door slam and Zero came bounding toward us barking as if he had never seen a person before.

Becky followed, and before I had even shown my first visitor my house, she was about to meet my neighbor. Zero smelled the fresh blood of a newcomer and ran to Justine. I wasn't sure how she would react and held my breath as he hurtled toward her.

There was nothing I could do about their meeting. After prowling the trails and streams of Plumas National Forest, I had a strange apprehension of dogs. Many hikers insisted on walking dogs off-leash. Some were better trained than others and most were fine, but the approaching hiker had no idea what was going through the dog's head. Their reactions ranged from affectionate to mad. The worst was when an unleashed dog approached one on a leash.

My worries faded when she crouched down and embraced him. After licking her face, Zero tucked his rear end into her body and presented his butt. She laughed and he absorbed the attention. I feared I had lost my drinking buddy until he suddenly realized I was standing there and came over.

"Don't y'all mind the dog," Becky said, coming toward us.

I could see by the look on her face that she was enjoying this and guessed that her fellow conspirator, Mariposa, the receptionist for the headquarters building, would be extending a dinner invitation to us in the morning. The coconut telegraph would be burning up tonight.

"Becky, this is Justine."

The women nodded to each other.

"Nice to meet you," Justine said, returning her attention to Zero, who had resumed pushing his butt against her leg.

"Damned dog's an embarrassment. He seems to like you though," Becky said.

For the first time in history, I thanked the mosquitos for finding us. I slapped my neck. "Bugs are bad. We're gonna head in," I said. After saying quick goodbyes and dodging the swarms of bugs, we made it to the house.

"Make yourself at home. I'll take the couch," I said. This had been our sleeping arrangement when I had stayed in her apartment. "I've got a couple of beers and some chips if you like."

"I'm good, and we need to get an early start in the morning so I can get to work by five." She came over and pecked my cheek.

The sparks were there, but before I could react, she'd gone into the bedroom and shut the door. She didn't slam it but closed it gently. I felt foolish judging her intentions based on how the door was closed, but when the light came on I smiled seeing the large gap where it was slightly ajar. Not that I was going to do anything about it, but it was a positive sign.

I lay down on the couch trying to find sleep, but it eluded me. With Justine in the next room and the faceless woman etched in my brain, I tossed and turned for what felt like hours.

At some point I must have dozed off. I smelled the coffee before I opened my eyes. Cracking them, I saw sunlight already streaming into the room and Justine in the kitchen. She was wearing one of my Park Service shirts.

"That's a better look on you than me," I said.

"That would be a matter of perspective." She handed me a cup of coffee. "Looks pretty nice out."

I remembered she had to be at work later and started moving, trying to disguise the obvious signs that I wasn't a morning person. I was all right after a few minutes, but the transition between sleep and life was hard. I pulled it together, sucking down two cups of coffee in the process, and a half hour later, we were headed out the door.

"The body was just around that bend," I said, pointing to the deep-water cut between the two mangrove-covered islands straight off the dock. I had to force myself to pay attention to the wind and water instead of watching her bend over and release the bowline from the cleat. They say a river is different every time you step into it; the ocean is that times four after adding in the tides and current.

The wind had the boat pinned against the dock, and I tried to remember the proper technique from my Chapman piloting book.

Before I could recall it, Zero came bounding out of the house. Becky followed with Jamie on her hip.

"I'd be watching the wind if I were y'all. Supposed to blow later," she said.

Justine was down on one knee petting Zero. "Just going into the little lagoon there to check something out."

"Ray has a honey hole in there. Pulls a half-dozen lobsters at a time from that cut there. Current running as it is, I expect you could too."

Justine stood. "Lobster, for real? That would be awesome."

"I'll go fetch you a tickle stick and net," Becky said, handing Jamie to me.

With the two-year-old in my arms, we walked toward the path and I called Zero over. I placed the baby on the dog's back, and we did what Jamie liked most—Zero rides. Seconds later he was shrieking with joy. I held his back and Zero walked proudly forward. Becky scoffed at our shenanigans and handed Justine the two-foot-long stick and net.

"Y'all know how to use these?"

"Sure. I usually dive for them," she said, and turned to me. "Do you have a mask and fins?"

I was getting out of my element. Of course, I knew it was two weeks into lobster season, but it was my first year there and I hadn't had a chance to hunt for them yet. "Sure. May be big on you."

She looked at Becky and realizing that she was almost my size turned back before the woman understood her appraisal. "We'll make it work."

I handed Jamie off to Becky and went back to the boat. Becky followed and went for the bowline. I saw what she was doing and called for Justine to come aboard. After I started the engine, Becky released the line but kept a wrap around the cleat. Setting the throttle to reverse, I backed away from the dock, using the bow as a pivot point. When I had the stern into the wind, Becky released the bight and tossed the line onto the deck. I continued to back away until I could move forward without getting blown back into the dock. I pushed the throttle forward, and Becky waved and Zero barked as we moved away from the dock.

With the wind blowing in our faces, I could feel the drag on the boat as we idled into the cut. Once we turned the corner into the small lagoon, the mangroves gave us shelter and the water settled to a light chop. "Right there," I said, pointing to the spot where I'd found the body. Ten feet before I reached it, I dropped the Power-Pole and cut the engine.

"How deep is it?" Justine asked.

The usually-turquoise water was off-colored due to the wind. "Five feet here," I said. "Must be near high tide; it was only three feet yesterday."

"Mind if I take a look?" she asked, stripping off her shirt. A minute later, clad in bra and panties, she took the mask and fins and slid over the side.

As she finned around on the surface, I wondered if she was able to see anything in the murky water, but a minute later I saw one leg lift, and barely making a ripple, she slid under the surface. Time stood still as I watched the water. It was definitely over a minute before I saw her blond hair and then her huge smile.

"She was right. There's lobster there." She took a few strokes toward the boat. "Toss me the net and stick."

I handed them down to her and without a word, she swam off again. It took her a minute to find the spot, and she stayed on the surface for a moment, catching her breath. Suddenly her body inverted. She flipped into a pike and disappeared. She wasn't gone long this time, and when she came up I saw something in the net.

She swam to the boat. "You okay if I grab a few more?"

I wasn't sure how this would play out with Martinez if we were discovered and didn't know what to say. The lagoon had only one entry, and I figured I would hear a boat approach long before it reached us. "Sure, go for it," I called back, taking the net and dumping the lobster on the deck.

While she went back for another try, I looked around the lagoon, feeling paranoid that even if we weren't spotted, I wasn't doing anything to find out who the Jane Doe was. Justine broke the surface with the net raised triumphantly over her head, and distracted now, I looked around the deck of the boat. The built-in fish boxes were crammed full of gear. I found a bucket, which I filled halfway with seawater, and placed the lobster in it. By the time I had finished she was back with another.

I didn't want to be the mean old dad, pulling the plug on the party, but I was getting nervous. We had four lobsters now and she had gone back for more. I missed her entry and was looking around the lagoon when she surfaced. From the expression on her face, I knew right away that the lobstering was over for the day.

6

STEVEN BECKER

A KURT HUNTER MYSTERY

BACKWATER BAY

JUSTINE PULLED the dark object toward the boat, fighting the weight as it dragged her down. At first, I thought it was another body. Feeling like an idiot for just staring at her struggling to keep her head above water without losing whatever she had, I pulled up the Power-Pole and carefully idled over to her. She approached the transom dragging the object behind her, then it disappeared and she swam toward the transom. I checked to make sure the engine was in neutral but thought better of it and shut it off when she reached the ladder. She hung on for a minute and caught her breath.

"I found the gear," she panted. "It's below the boat."

"You want me to get in and help?"

"No, just toss me a line and I'll hook it up."

I grabbed a line from the forward hold and uncoiled it. "Ready?"

"Yup. Hand me the end and feed it back," she said, taking the end of the line.

I fed the line back to her until she stopped and then, figuring the depth was about ten feet, let a few more coils drop into the water. She swam in a circle and when she had found her spot, she dropped under the surface. It took less time for her to tie the line to the gear than to bag a lobster and she was quickly back at the boat. I grabbed her hand, not failing to notice the water beading off all the right parts of her body, and helped her aboard.

"Come on. Let's see what we have," she said, pulling the line.

"Just keep the slack out," I said, and went to the helm, where I started the engine, and followed the line until it was vertical in the water. I had learned a few boating lessons in my time there, and one was how to lift an anchor. Lifting the gear from the bottom was the same concept.

Together we pulled the surprisingly heavy load to the surface. I saw the tank, and then the buoyancy compensator hanging below it. Once it was secured, I turned to her. "Do we have to do anything special to protect it?"

Justine thought for a second. "If it's been in the water as long as I suspect, there's no forensic evidence left, but we should do the best we can. Let's just get it aboard and have a look."

We pulled the line closer to the boat and when I could reach the air valve, I grabbed it and swung the tank and BC over the gunwale and onto the boat. Water slopped onto the deck and we stood there looking at the gear as a handful of crabs crawled out of the weight pockets. It wasn't my call what to do next, and I waited for Justine to decide.

"It's a mess, but we still need to preserve it. Do you have any garbage bags or a tarp?"

"At the house," I said.

"We should probably head back and get this processed," she said. The enthusiasm that had shown on her face after catching the lobsters was gone. In its place was another look, a cross between worried and excited. She looked something like a kid with a new toy who wasn't quite sure how to use it.

"Martinez might be a problem with this. You being out here

and coming back with evidence. Can we go ashore after he leaves?"

She thought about it for a second. "The sooner we get it back, the better, and I have to be at work at five."

I saw her glance at the equipment lying on the deck and realized she was anxious. "I'll get Mariposa to give me a heads-up on what's going on at the office." The Jamaican receptionist was my only real ally at headquarters. Martinez and his confidant, counterpart, or whatever she was, Susan McLeash, were paper-pushing, by-the-book bureaucrats. The other officers who lived and worked on the islands were mostly responsible for the campgrounds and day-use areas. I had some contact with them, but our paths seldom crossed.

"Okay. I wouldn't want to start trouble for you," she said.

I felt like I was making the wrong decision, not facing up to my boss, but let it go as we approached the dock. The wind was in my favor now, and well before we got there, I asked Justine to put out the fenders and ready the dock lines. Taking my time, I stopped a good thirty feet away to see what the wind and current were going to do and eased the boat against the dock. It had been so well done that not even Zero noticed our presence until Justine set foot on the dock.

He came bounding out of the house, barking and running toward us. After he skidded to a stop, Justine reached down and petted him while I unloaded the lobsters onto the dock.

Becky appeared in the doorway smiling. She came over and gave me a quick lesson in how to clean them. Putting on thick gloves to protect my hands, I twisted the tails from the bodies and used the pointy end of one of their antennae to clean out the innards. When I was done, I carried the tails into the house and put them in a bowl in the refrigerator. Justine followed me in with Zero on her heels.

"I was thinking we could have some lunch," she said. "Maybe have a look at the gear too, before we bag it."

I was all in favor of anything that would kill a little time before we went back and also let me spend some time with her. "Sounds good. I'll go call Mariposa and light the grill."

"I'm going to grab a shower," she said, heading to the bedroom.

I was feeling good about having company here and I went outside to start the grill. It was then my phone rang and my day started going downhill.

"What the hell were you doing in the lagoon where you found the woman for the last few hours?"

I had to hold the phone away from my ear, Martinez was screaming so loud. Several thoughts crossed my mind. The first was the question of why he was tracking me. From previous experience, I knew the GPS on the Park Service boats tracked and recorded our movements, but why was he so concerned with what I was doing that he had to monitor me? Or was watching his agents from the comfort of his desk his idea of doing his job?

"I thought there might be something in there to help establish her identity." It was close to true.

"Once again, Hunter, as soon as the body goes to Miami-Dade, it's theirs. Now, seeing as I can't trust you to do your job, I want a written schedule submitted by five o'clock this afternoon detailing which areas you will be patrolling and when for the rest of the week. The schedule will need to be corroborated with written reports. And, by the way, I know you've got company out there."

It was one thing to know about where the boat was, but how did he know I had someone here? I had to assume, if he knew that much, he knew who she was as well. I told him I would be in the office in a few hours. The sliding glass door from the living room opened and I disconnected before he replied. Justine stood there, and I forgot the call for a second. With her wet hair down to her shoulders and my favorite T-shirt looking a lot better on her than it ever would on me, I had to fight myself to stop staring.

"Who were you talking to?" she asked.

"Martinez, who somehow knows that you're here and we spent the morning in the lagoon."

"That puts a damper on the party," she said. She walked toward me, took the tongs from my hand, and turned the lobster tails. "I saw some salad stuff in the fridge."

The lobster was great, and I tried to put on a happy face as we talked about the morning. There were promises of more adventures to come and I was feeling really good until our plates were empty and we stared at each other with that "what now?" look. "I have to do some paperwork for Martinez. If you want I can take you back and do it there."

"I'd like to have a quick look at the gear before we go," she said.

It was already starting to stink when we hauled the tank and BC onto the dock. I thought about hosing it down but knew it would harm any evidence. As it turned out, Justine wasn't as concerned, probably knowing the salt water had already destroyed everything. She hosed the gear off and started disassembling it. Scuba equipment was foreign to me, so I left her to it and went inside to make my plan for Martinez. I had a pile of tourist maps of the park that I gave to lost or grounded boaters after highlighting the shoals and navigation aids. With one of these, I took a Sharpie and marked off five equal sections. Adding the days of the week to each, I folded it up and put it in my pocket. That was my plan.

Back on the dock, Zero was hovering over the gear and Justine, trying to decide which was more interesting.

"Want me to get rid of him?"

"Nope, he's my buddy."

"Okay, but if he's in the way . . ."

She shook her head. "Look, I found this in one of the BC pockets."

"It's just a socket wrench," I said. "And what's that?" She held out something covered in algae. I took it from her and turned it in my hand. It was some sort of mounting plate with two predrilled holes. I figured it measured about six by three inches and brushed the green gunk off of it.

"I'm not sure. I think she was some kind of commercial diver."

"How do you figure?"

"Divers try to carry only what they need. Look at all the clips on the vest," she said, toying with the brass clips attached to rings sewn into the vest. "There are half a dozen here, and they look well used. Most recreational divers would only have one or two." She held one of the hooks up in the daylight and I could see the wear on it.

I looked at the BC with a new eye now. "Does the other gear tell you anything?"

"Regulator is well used but pretty straightforward. There is no octopus, which reinforces my theory."

It was good to know we had a theory. "What's an octopus?"

"You really need me, don't you? If you're gonna be Ranger Rick out here, you need to learn some stuff."

I couldn't argue that and let it pass.

"An octopus is an alternate air source. If your dive buddy runs out of air, the extra regulator allows them to breathe off your tank."

"Got it, and the fact that there isn't one means whoever used this equipment didn't dive with a buddy. Where would you dive alone?"

She laid out the BC and I could see discoloration. "A lot of commercial divers work alone: cleaning or making repairs at dock. That might explain the wetsuit as well. If she were working under barnacle-covered hulls, she would want it for protection." She continued her inspection.

"Looks like wear and tear, not anything from trauma," I said.

"Yes, like she was rubbing up against something." She turned the BC over and we saw the torn waist belt and straps. "That pretty much confirms Sid's propeller theory. Cut right through the straps."

My knees were starting to hurt from squatting and I got up and paced the dock. She had set the tank off to the side and it caught my eye. The thigh-high cylinder had a milled metal finish and worn stickers on it. I moved closer to examine them and felt Justine behind me. There were at least a dozen stickers, some worn to just their base color by the BC straps. Several were from gear companies, but one looked official. "What's this?" I asked.

"Oh, wow. It's the inspection sticker. I should have thought about that. Every year the tank needs to get a visual inspection, or VIP. There should be a dive shop's name on it."

I looked closer and saw the shop's name. The address was in Miami Beach. "I'm thinking we finally have a legit lead. Whoever inspected the tank might know our Jane Doe."

"Let's go. If you can get past Martinez, we have enough time to stop by before I have to go to work."

"Deal," I said, and started picking up the gear and loaded it on the boat, thinking about how to deal with Martinez.

"You just show him your map and distract him, I'll take care of the gear."

There was nothing like a little collusion to bring two people together, and with the gear loaded we took off for the headquarters building.

STEVEN BECKER

A KURT HUNTER MYSTERY

BACKWATER BAY

SOMETIMES WHEN YOU don't overthink something, it just works. I wish I could say that about my relationships. I had already wrecked one, and looking over at Justine, I promised myself I'd be more careful. They said women were like boats. Maybe if I mastered one, I could master the other. I was feeling pretty good about the boat thing when the center-console slid right into the slip without incident. I was two for two today, and it gave a good boost to my confidence. I guess Becky and Ray's coaching was paying off.

"Give me a minute to get inside," I said to Justine, leaving her aboard. She huddled under the T-top to avoid the rain that had just started. We had decided to leave the scuba gear in plain sight, and if Martinez said anything, the story was that Justine had been diving on the site and the equipment was hers. Hopefully, he'd be so focused on me that he wouldn't see the torn straps on the BC. As it turned out, the ruse was not necessary.

During the summer months, it rained almost every day, and today was no exception. We had seen the large anvil cloud hovering above the mainland on the way in. There were no visible lightning strikes or special weather advisories on the VHF, so we continued in. It had started sprinkling when we passed the first marker for the channel leading to the park headquarters. The T-top and windshield had kept us dry until we were in the slip, but as we'd unloaded the equipment onto the dock the heavens had opened.

The summer squalls common to the tropics were different from the storms out west. In the Sierra, you had your big storms. They came off the ocean, bringing high winds and lots of precipitation, but nothing like the sheeting rain and violent thunderstorms here. Within seconds it was raining so hard, I could barely see Justine standing three feet away through the curtain of fat drops.

"I have to get the keys to the truck," I said, leaving her and the gear under an overhang by the entrance. I went inside, shook off like a dog, and went to Mariposa's desk. Seeing me shiver, she thankfully kept the conversation short and handed me the keys.

Back outside, the rain was still sheeting down. "Let's make a run for it," I said, grabbing the tank. She picked up the rest of the gear and followed. The drops stung as we passed the entrance to the building and I looked up at Martinez's window. It was obscured by the storm. I could only hope that if I couldn't see him, he couldn't see me.

I unlocked the doors with the key fob when we were still ten feet from the truck. Tossing the gear in the bed of the pickup, we fell into the front seats. We took a quick look at each other, both drenched to the bone, which started a laughing fit that lasted several minutes and was only broken when the rain let up and we could hear ourselves.

"Can you hang out for a minute and let me take my beating?" The humidity from the storm and our wet bodies had created its own weather system in the small truck. It got even steamier when she leaned in, surprising me. Her face was blurred by the water in my eyes and the cloud in the cab, and I almost missed it when her lips hit mine.

It was our first real kiss, and I could only hope Martinez didn't have security cameras back there to watch. Just the thought made me nervous, and I pulled away. "Rain's let up. I better go before he sees the boat."

"Right. I'll be here," she said, turning on the heater.

I put my game face on and headed toward the building, hoping the rain had been too heavy for Martinez to see anything.

Mariposa took one look at me when I walked back in and directed me to the men's room to clean up. There was not much I could do about my soaking-wet clothes. I dried my face with a paper towel and smoothed down my hair.

My clothes clung to my skin, sending a shiver down my spine as I walked through the artificially cooled air and up the stairs. Susan was at her desk, as usual, and I gave her a quick wave, not surprised when she looked down at her computer screen as if she were too busy to acknowledge me. Though our job titles were the same, our approaches were totally opposite. We both held the title of special agent, though hers could have read "special agent in charge of paperwork." I loathed her approach. I loved my job but hated the bureaucracy that came with it—the action was out in the field. Thinking about the report Martinez had asked for, I pulled my hastily drawn schedule from my pocket. What had taken me about two minutes to produce would have been a day's work for Susan, and after she spent hours modifying it every day, there would be no time to actually follow it.

His door was open and he waved me in. I sat and pulled the paper from the front pocket of my shirt. It was damp and I unfolded it, hoping Martinez wouldn't hold the storm against me. It was curious how he was always on the phone when I entered his office, and that he seemed to purposefully cross the line where the length of the call became rude. I smoothed the map out on my wet pants and waited.

"You're not going to tell me that that's your attempt at a schedule?" he asked after he hung up and grunted a greeting.

I had no choice but to hand the paper to him. Without allowing a drop of water to land on him or his desk, he handed it back. Reaching for a file folder, he pulled out several papers stapled together and handed them to me. "This is a schedule."

I took the papers and looked at the neatly typed report. It was Susan's work of course. "I don't have a printer on the island," I said, knowing it was a feeble excuse.

"This is an office, Hunter." He waved his hands around. "There's actually one with your name on it down the hall."

Unless attendance there was mandatory, I wouldn't be stuck in the closet-sized room. I could have whined that Susan's office was four times the size but knew it would only further enrage him. "Right. I'll do better next week," I said, hoping I would have a reprieve.

"If you'd stop sticking your nose in every damned mangrove bush in the park, we wouldn't have a problem. The ecosystem here will clean everything up for us—if you let it. Your job is to pull tourists off the flats and make sure no one gets killed out there. If they're already dead, I don't care."

I noticed him glance at one of the pair of computer monitors on his desk and turned in my chair. From my position, I could just see the monitor and its checkerboard pattern of surveillance cameras.

"Right. I'll be better about that." That was how he knew I had company. I wondered what he could see on the island and if my own house was monitored. Surely, I thought, the dock would be, and if he was here and watching, he would have seen the equipment we had recovered—and the lobster.

A loud crash shook the building and we both turned to the

windows. Thunder boomed and a brilliant blue lightning bolt looked like it struck the parking lot across the street. It was quiet for a second and then the deluge started again.

"Careful with the boat in this weather. Maybe ride out the storm in that office of yours and get me a schedule. Susan would be happy to help."

"Good idea," I said. I would have done anything to get out of there, even if it meant asking Susan for help. "I'll do that." I rose to leave and saw his glance drift back to the monitor. "I've got some errands to run, mind if I check out a vehicle when I'm done with the schedule?"

He nodded. As long as he got his paperwork and could monitor the park from the comfort of his office, I don't think he cared about anything else. I left the office and stopped at Susan's door. "Boss says you can help me make a schedule?"

"I see you got a girlfriend."

There was just a tinge of venom in her voice. I looked across the neat desk at her. She was sitting in her regulation uniform, with everything just perfect, including her hair, which was as flat and polished as her gun belt. She was clearly not my type. Not that I would have crossed the line if she was. Justine might even have been a little too close to work for a relationship, but I had already rationalized that and decided that since she worked for another jurisdiction it was okay.

She must have noticed my evaluation. "Just log in to the network and you'll find a folder marked—get this—*Schedules*," she said. "Do a little copy-and-paste work and you're good to go."

I thanked her and walked to the other end of the hall, where my broom closet was located. Unlike hers and Martinez's, it was an interior office, with no window. The furniture consisted of a chair and a bare desk facing a blank wall. I sat in the chair and stared at the dark computer monitor.

I sent a quick text to Justine saying that I was waylaid for a few minutes. Reaching forward, I turned on the computer and monitor and waited for them to start up. I entered my password and pulled the chair closer. Paperwork was my enemy, but I knew my way around computers. After locating the network drive, I found the folder where Susan said it would be and opened her latest schedule. It took less than a minute to realize it was fiction. I had actually been fishing some of the places she was scheduled to patrol.

If this was what Martinez wanted, I could grant his wish. Following her example, I filled in a blank form with places and times. I glanced at my watch noticing it had been almost a half hour since I left Justine in the truck. Feeling guilty, I opened my email program and sent Martinez the schedule. On my way to the stairs, he called out thanking me. I smiled. This wasn't all it was going to take to get him off my back, but it was a start.

Downstairs at the reception desk, Mariposa offered her usual invitation to dinner and that good rum she would only allow her husband to break out for special guests. I would have to go one of these days just so the poor soul could finally taste it.

With the heat on high, I found Justine asleep when I got back to the truck. Trying not to wake her, I pulled out of the lot. The storm was gone now, leaving a brilliant sky behind and every rut and pothole full of water. Most of the trip was against rush hour, but the traffic was slow following the storm. The rain was slowly soaking through the porous limestone and into the aquifer. I was finally driving the speed limit as I passed downtown Miami on the 836. I continued onto the MacArthur Causeway, passing some bazillion-dollar houses on the left and the cruise ship pier on the right. When we hit South Beach, Justine woke up and looked around. Before she could ask where we were, I turned south onto Alton Road and found the address on the inspection sticker located inside a marina on the right.

Grabbing the tank from the bed of the truck we headed across the parking lot, dodging the massive puddles left from the storm. To the right, I saw a red and white dive flag flying from a pole above one of the buildings and we headed toward it.

By the time we reached the shop my arms were aching from carrying the tank. The entrance was on the marina side and I couldn't help but notice the money sitting in the water in front of me as I dragged the scarred steel cylinder through the door.

A chime sounded when we entered and I looked around the store. The front at least was more of a boutique selling shirts, hats, and sunglasses than what I expected a dive shop would look like. I guessed the rent was high enough there that one couldn't be a purist. Wondering if we had been noticed, we walked toward a pair of swinging doors blocking entry to a back room. It sounded like a big compressor was running and I called out a greeting. A minute later, the noise died and a thirty-something man walked toward us.

"What can I do for you?" he asked.

I had my uniform on. There would be no small talk. "You know who this belongs to?" I asked, not knowing where else to begin.

He took the tank and rolled it until the inspection sticker faced him. "This is Abbey's tank," he said, brushing the milled steel.

8

"DOES ABBEY HAVE A LAST NAME?" I asked.

"Give me a minute and I'll check. We keep copies of all our regulars' certification cards on file," he said, and disappeared behind the swinging doors.

I heard the compressor start back up and assumed he was doing double duty, filling tanks while he talked to us. The sticker on the tank had turned out to be a solid lead, and I could tell Justine was as excited as I was. Her phone rang and she motioned with her eyes that she was going outside to take the call. The shop was noisy with the compressor running. Alone in the store, I wandered the aisles trying to figure out how all the different pieces and parts of the scuba equipment went together.

"Thinking about learning?" Justine asked, surprising me. I hadn't heard her come back in.

"Actually, I should." I picked up two stainless steel parts and examined them.

"We should take a road trip to Key Largo. Alicia and T. J. will take care of you."

I had met them several weeks ago. "Sounds good." I noticed a change in her. "Something wrong?"

"Just work. That was my boss asking when I'd be in. Apparently, we've had a busy day. You okay if I take off?"

"Sure, let's just get the info from Mr. Dive Dude and I'll drive you back."

"No need. I told him if he wanted me to come in early he should send a patrol car to pick me up."

I would have rather had her beside me. "How about if I swing by later and we look at the gear?"

"That would be good. Text me first though."

The compressor was still running and I looked back to the saloon doors. There was no sign of the guy, so I walked Justine to the door and said goodbye. It was a work goodbye, like two partners splitting up to take different assignments, not the date kind of goodbye that I had in mind. I watched her walk around the building and went back inside.

The dive guy was behind the counter digging through a file when I came back in. I felt awkward standing in front of him. This kind of work was new to me and I had to figure out the right demeanor to present; too much or too little attitude would not get me the information I needed. I decided to take the mellow approach since he was working on what I asked for and took a step back to give him some room.

A few minutes later, he pulled a paper out and looked up. "Bentley's her last name." He laid it on the counter.

I stepped closer and picked it up. The certification card had a picture that, if you squinted, could have been of the victim. Maybe there was some kind of facial recognition software we could run to confirm it, but the cheekbones and eyes were the same. It looked like Abbey Bentley was our Jane Doe.

"Mind if I take a copy of that?" I asked.

"I guess I should ask for a warrant." He paused and I saw the fear in his eyes. "Look, she's a good kid. Works for Bottoms Up, cleaning ships' hulls. Can you tell me what you're after?"

We were probably the same age, but I expected the uniform lent me an air of authority. "What's your name?"

"Laird," he said.

I wondered for a second if you were destined to do this kind of job if you had a surfer name, then decided it was not the kind of detective work that was going to help. "I need to find her family," I said, thinking it was a nice way of saying I needed to contact the next of kin.

"She comes in here for air fills all the time. Pretty sure most of her work was out of the marina here. We talked some, but it was mostly just dive stuff; nothing about her friends or family."

"So, the copy?"

"I don't know. I could lose my job."

My phone was still in my hand. "Here, you were in back filling tanks and never saw this." I stepped forward and took a picture of the paper. A brochure for their certification program lay on the counter.

He must have seen me looking at it. "You can take it. We can hook you up if you want to check it out," he said.

"Thanks." I picked it up and stuck it in my pocket as I looked at the paper. "You know where her address is?"

"The Gables," he said. "Out by the U."

I thanked him, not really sure what he was talking about but figuring Google would take it from there.

I left the shop with the tank in hand, thinking I had a new friend. I decided to use one of the half-dozen wheelbarrows lined up on the dock instead of hauling it this time. Back at the truck, I slung the cylinder into the bed with the BC and climbed into the front seat. Opening the picture on my phone, I looked at the head shot of Abbey Bentley and enlarged it. It was a little creepy looking at a dead woman, but I was just trying to make some kind of connection. I entered the address into the maps app and set the phone on the passenger seat.

I wasn't the seasoned law enforcement veteran my résumé made me appear. My reputation from finding the pot grow was misleading. It wasn't police work that had landed me on the front page of every paper from Idaho to Mexico City. It was fishing. For most of the year, the small towns and foothills of the Sierra Nevada were quiet. Meth was a problem there as anywhere, but the labs were usually on private property, not on national forest land. Six months a year, most of the forest was under a blanket of snow. The cross-country skiers and snowshoers were not exactly the criminal demographic. Snowmobilers were a little more radical, but aside from dangerous stunts or crossing into areas where the machines were prohibited, they were no trouble. Summer was the busy season when illegal dredging or claim jumping and poaching kept me busy. In half a dozen years I'd had no dead bodies and few arrests.

I figured I was in the big leagues now with two bodies only weeks apart. The first had been a refugee. He was never identified, but the discovery of the body had led to the takedown of a human smuggling enterprise. The second was Abbey Bentley.

Laird had said something about her working for Bottoms Up. Half expecting a strip bar, I punched the name into the search engine and found Abbey's place of employment. The website said Bottoms Up was a business employing scuba divers to clean boat bottoms at the owner's slip. Looking around at the hundreds of boats visible from here, I expected there was plenty of work. The address appeared as a link, which I clicked and opened a map. The app informed me that the business was closed, but the office was in this complex.

I decided on a quick look before I went to Abbey's house. Locking the truck, I followed the walking directions until I had completed two circles. Frustrated, I put the phone in my pocket and, resorting to some old-fashioned police work, asked the closest man who looked like he worked there. He pointed me down a dock with two shack-like buildings near the end. I walked out and saw the marketing genius of the owner. It was like the hot-body maid thing, except with hot girls cleaning boat bottoms in bikinis.

The sign showed the scantily clad bottom of a young lady in the foreground while she cleaned a boat bottom. It did attract your attention, and if I'd had the kind of money spread out on the water in front of me, I would have called them for my boat—no references required. I walked to the sliding glass door that served the office and pulled the handle. The app hadn't lied and the business was indeed closed.

"You needin' your bottom cleaned?"

I turned around and found myself face-to-face with a man. After a quick eyeball, I decided his name had to be Biff. If there was ever the stereotypical preppy boat guy, I was looking at him. "Just had a few questions."

"I'm the owner, if there's something I can help you with." He brushed past me, pulling a key chain out of his pocket, and opened the door.

He must have noticed my uniform because he almost pulled me inside. I guessed I wasn't his ideal customer and he wanted me out of sight. It was a small office with a room air conditioner barely winning the battle with the August humidity. A small desk was off to the side. The focal point for the room was the employee pictures. All bottoms up and smiling. The place had that Mexican tourist trap kind of feel and my skin started to crawl.

"What can we do for the Park Service? If y'all are wanting your bottoms cleaned, we're a little on the pricey side," he said with a smirk. "Get what you pay for if you know what I mean."

I half expected a wink with that last line and was ready to land my Park Service fist on his well-tanned cheeks. Somehow I found it offensive that he was talking about my dead body like that. Instead, I breathed deeply and turned away from him. There were a dozen women on the wall, and I tried to focus on their faces, looking for Abbey. She was in the bottom row. I pulled out my phone and opened the picture of her cert card. It was her.

"Can you tell me about that girl?" I asked, pointing to her.

"She's one of our best. Been around a while and has a slew of regulars." This time he did wink, and I clenched my fists, trying to restrain myself.

"How about an employment file?" I asked. I didn't want his personal views.

"We run a legal enterprise here. All on the up-and-up, if you get my drift. Anything that happens on the side doesn't go through here."

He was getting defensive now and I needed to change tactics. "When was the last time you saw her?"

He scratched his head. "Mostly what I do is email. I don't have much contact."

"When was the last time you emailed her?" I asked.

"Something gone wrong?"

"Just getting some background. I got no axe to grind with you. I'm just trying to find her."

He pulled his phone out and sat down by the desk. "Give me a minute."

It was painful watching him fumble through the screens, one finger peck at a time.

Finally, he looked up. "Been a few weeks." He ran his hand through his hair. "We don't run a nine-to-five operation here. Usually, when I get a call, unless the owner requests someone, I put it out to all the girls. First one that answers gets the work. This one was a family deal so it just went to her. It was the *Big Bang* she was cleaning. The business still went through me because I've got a non-compete clause here at the marina."

That sounded like a crappy way to treat your employees and their families. He must have sensed my disgust.

"Hey. I got rent and bills. Insurance too," he said.

I sensed the conversation going backward. "No worries. Can you give me the dates and some contact information to reach you?" I asked, pulling my notepad out of my pocket.

He seemed to get a little jiggy when I started to actually write things down.

"Something happen to her?"

I thought I saw a bead of sweat pop out of his forehead and I decided to push just a little harder. "You might say that." The reaction surprised me so much, I almost wrote *Suspect #1* on my pad. Instead, I took one of his business cards from the cheap Plexiglas holder on his desk and handed him one of mine. "If you think of anything, give me a call." From the look on his face, I knew that was wasted. Biff was not going to be calling.

9

STEVEN BECKER

A KURT HUNTER MYSTERY

BACKWATER BAY

IT WAS ALMOST dark when I left the marina. Heading back over the MacArthur Causeway, I reached the mainland and turned left onto US 1. Although I wasn't an expert on Miami's neighborhoods, there was a clear line between the upscale Coconut Grove and the older Coral Gables. The streets became closer together and the houses were older and on smaller lots. I turned off South Dixie at Le Jeune Road and drove several blocks past the careful land-scaping attempting to conceal the Water and Sewer Department facility.

Slowing down to search for the address, between the dive tank rattling around the bed of the small white pickup and the Park Service logo on the doors, I was far from discreet, and I caught several looks from dog walkers and joggers. I tried to ignore them and scanned the street for the address on Abbey's certification card.

An ad had popped up on my map screen when I entered the address asking if I was interested in buying the house at that loca-tion. Out of curiosity, I clicked on it and saw the house was for sale with an asking price just north of six hundred thousand. Looking at the neighborhood now, I couldn't see it. The houses were mostly old ranches on small lots. As I approached, I did see several nice two-story homes being built. The land was apparently worth more than the houses to the developers trying to rebuild the neighborhood. At this kind of price range, I started to wonder if this was her parents' house. It was certainly not the kind of neighborhood a boat cleaner could afford, even with Biff's business plan.

I ended up finding it by the FOR SALE sign in the front yard and pulled over across from the house. Now I took a minute to look at it before filing it away. I was close enough to a streetlight to see the same inverted bikini-clad bottom as the one on his sign staring back at me. I did notice his name was Gordon. He looked more like a Biff, but I knew I had better start addressing him as his mother did—maybe Gordo, or Gordy, I thought. While I was doing homework, I pulled up the picture with the copy of Abbey's certification card again and double-checked the address against the faded painted tiles on the mailbox; it matched. I looked at the house. Several lights were on inside.

I left the truck in the street, figuring parking in the driveway would make the visit somehow more official. In truth, this was the second investigative call of my career and I was feeling my way through it. Leaving the standard-issue Park Service ball cap on the passenger seat, I ran my hands through my hair and walked across the street. As I went up the uneven path, I could see the property was neglected. The tropical landscaping and Spanish-style architecture of the old house were both in need of some TLC. A dog barked, catching me by surprise, and just before I pressed the flamingo doorbell, the door opened.

A face peered out and squinted at me. It was an odd squint.

"Ma'am, my name is Kurt Hunter, with the National Park Service," I said, extending my hand.

"Holly Sanders," the woman said, offering her hand, palm down.

I took it and gave her one of my business cards, figuring this wasn't a show-your-badge kind of visit. "I'm looking for Abbey Bentley," I said.

She gave me a look that I couldn't quite place. "Why don't we talk inside."

We walked through the foyer, over frayed antique carpets blanketing Southern yellow pine flooring that was in need of refinishing, and went to the kitchen. The walls were plastered, but it looked like the fake drywall texture that was so popular now. The furniture was mostly craftsman, though old. I followed her into the newly-remodeled kitchen that was too IKEA for the house, and she offered me a seat at a raised bar.

"Very nice house," I said, more to open her up than meaning it. Northern California winters were long, cold, and rainy. I had spent the last half-dozen winters remodeling our old farmhouse, becoming an acceptable carpenter in the process. Thinking about that brought memories of Janet and Allie and the bomb that had destroyed everything. I tried to focus on Holly and push my past aside.

She must have noticed something. "Can I get you a glass of water, or something stronger maybe?"

It looked like she had already been into the something stronger. I declined. "Water would be great, thanks," I said, trying to pull myself together. She turned, got a glass from a cabinet, and filled it using a small spout on the sink. I took it and thanked her. Taking a sip, I tried to figure out where to start. Her last name was different from Abbey's, but I noticed a resemblance. "Are you and Abbey related?"

"She's my niece," Holly said. "Is something wrong?"

I was getting into next-of-kin territory. Taking my phone from my pocket, I opened the picture of Abbey's cert card and pushed it across the counter. "Is this her?" I saw her hand tremble.

"Yes. Has something happened to her?"

"Ma'am, I'm not sure how to ask this, but how can I find her parents?"

Before she could answer, a door slammed. "Holly?"

She looked at me apologetically. "My husband."

Just as the words were out of her mouth, a man walked into the kitchen and eyed me suspiciously. I could tell right away that something was wrong. If you hang around the small foothill towns in Northern California long enough you can spot alcohol and drug users from a mile away. Abbey's uncle fell into both categories.

"Who the hell are you?"

I got up and extended my hand. "Kurt Hunter with the National Park Service."

He looked at Holly. "I told you not to answer the door for these fund-raising types. They can smell your money a mile away." He turned to me. "What are you saving today? Turtles, Flipper, or what?"

I was about to answer, but Holly cut me off. "Herb," she scolded him. "It's not like that. It's about Abbey."

I could see the change immediately and he staggered backward a few steps, grabbing the counter for support.

"Her parents?" I asked, trying to refocus the conversation.

"We've been looking after her for a long time," she said, moving toward her husband and putting an arm around him.

I guessed this was as good as it was going to get. My problem was, I had no idea what to do now. My training had covered how to break bad news and I guessed this was the time, but there was no positive identification, or even a chance for that with her crab-eaten face. I ran my hand through my hair and the answer came.

"I have some bad news," I started. "I think we have your niece in the medical examiner's office, but we have no positive identification."

"You come barging in here and tell us you think Abbey's dead, but you're not sure?" Herb said.

His body language had changed. The dazed and confused look was gone; he was confident now, and trying to take control of the situation, but it looked forced. "Did she live here?"

"We have an apartment out back that she rented," Holly said.

"I'd like to see it if I could," I said.

"I'd like to see a warrant," Herb said.

"Herb, we are going to cooperate," Holly told her husband.

It was starting to look like everyone related to this case was jiggy. I looked at Holly and asked the question again with my eyes, figuring old Herb was too far gone to notice. She led me through a back hallway. I glanced behind me and saw no sign of Herb. Before exiting the house, she grabbed a key hung from a small rope on a hook by the back door.

Their backyard was pretty plain and overgrown. It was clear they had spent what money they had to improve the inside. Behind a sprawling live oak was a small outbuilding. Holly went to the door and unlocked it with the key. I kept my distance, wanting her to have some space. A light turned on and I guessed that was my cue to enter.

My first reaction was that the place had been tossed, and I almost asked the question.

"She was not the greatest housekeeper," Holly said.

I stood just inside the door, trying to get my bearings, while Holly started to pick up. I call myself organized, though others have said I'm a bit of a neat freak. Despite my own leanings, this was beyond housekeeping. It looked like a pack of dogs had run through the small apartment, pulling books from shelves and knocking over furniture. The contents of the drawers were all over the floor. It looked like someone had been searching for something. Holly gave up after a minute, righted a fallen chair, and sat at the small table to the left of the front door. "Do you want to file a report?" I asked.

She gave me that squinty "I don't understand" look. I took a few steps into the small kitchen that was just beyond the table. To the right, on the other side of a hallway that serviced two doors, was the living area. I guessed the two doors were a bedroom and bathroom. I looked back at Holly and saw her head in her hands. Her body heaved and I could hear her inhale deeply. Not really sure what to do, I went to the sink and filled a glass with water, which I placed on the table in front of her. She didn't seem to notice.

Moving around the small apartment, I tried to get a sense of her niece. There were a lot of pictures, some framed and others just pinned to the wall. Many were underwater photographs. "Did she take these?" I asked.

Holly took a second to gather herself and turned to me. Her face was grief stricken and I immediately felt bad about asking. "She did. This is all hers," she said, drinking from the water glass. "Sorry."

"They're very good."

"Diving was her passion. I just wish she had stayed in school."

"Please, if you'd rather do this another time, I understand." I was in a place I'd never been in and wanted out. There was nothing else to be gained without a thorough search, which I felt was inappropriate.

She seemed to pull herself together. "No, whatever I can do to help."

I was uneasy but wanted something for having come this far. "A DNA sample would be helpful in identifying her. Maybe a hairbrush?" I asked.

She got up and went back to the bathroom, returning a minute later holding out a brush. I didn't have an evidence bag with me, so I took it by the handle, holding it gingerly and carefully keeping it away from anything that might contaminate it. I was heading to the kitchen to look for a baggie when Herb crashed through the door.

He stumbled in and said something unintelligible. Holly went to him, but he brushed her away. The chair that she had been sitting on toppled over and Holly ran past me out of the apartment, leaving me alone with Herb. I heard a crash and turned back to see he was on the floor, hopefully passed out. As long as Holly was safe, I decided there was nothing further to be gained there and showed myself out.

———

I STOPPED A FEW BLOCKS AWAY IN THE PARKING LOT OF A STRIP MALL occupied by a nail salon, yogurt shop, and liquor store—everything you'd ever need in South Florida. Staring at the neon beer signs, and wanting one more than I was ready to admit to myself, I went through my last two encounters, trying to get them straight in my head before I called Justine.

In the last few hours, I had gone from a sticker on a dive tank to an identity and two possible suspects. Maybe it was just my dislike for the men, but they were one and two on my short list. I had a long way to go to prove motive and opportunity, let alone how the murder was committed, but the alarm bells were ringing. It came back to me then that Sid had ruled the death a boating accident—not a homicide. Before I could start interrogating suspects, I had to find the cause of death.

"Hey," Justine answered on the second ring.

We were clearly into phase two of our relationship now that I had her cell number and didn't need to go through the Miami-Dade switchboard. "Hey, got time for dinner? I have some news."

"They've got me really busy here. Any chance you can pick up some takeout and come by?"

"You name it," I said, grateful for the opportunity to both see her and get into the lab.

An hour later, we sat in the crime lab with boxes of Thai takeout in front of us. It didn't quite measure up to the lobster we'd had for lunch and I still wanted that beer.

"So, tell me a story," she said, stuffing noodles into her mouth with chopsticks.

I wasn't as adept and used a fork for mine. Between bites, I told her about Bottoms Up and my meeting with Abbey's aunt and uncle. We finished and dumped the containers in the trash. It was time to ask the big question. "So," I started with a pregnant pause, "identifying the body. I didn't want to bring her aunt in to see her in this condition." Justine nodded and I continued. "I grabbed a hairbrush from the apartment. Can we run DNA on it to get a positive ID?"

"So," she mimicked me. "*We* need to talk to Sid. She's his baby as long as she's in the morgue."

This gave me the lead-in I needed. "And the 'cause of death' thing. I'm thinking there's more to this than a boating accident." Everything about the body, the gear, and the people involved was suspicious.

10

BACKWATER BAY

I WAS FEELING the adrenaline rush of progress and knew sleep wasn't coming. "Maybe I could go see Sid? I could grab a piece of hair or something and bring it back to compare to the brush?"

"I guess' we're just trying to establish her identity. I can compare the hair strands under a microscope and be pretty certain. At least sure enough to see if a DNA test is worthwhile."

"Cool," I said, starting for the door.

"Hold on there, Inspector. I better give him a call first."

I knew I was pushing the boundaries of her patience and made an excuse to use the bathroom to get away for a minute. I stared at myself in the mirror, and what I saw didn't match the way I felt. I'd been running for almost two days on only a few hours of sleep on the couch and it was starting to show. The stubble had filled in on my chin, and my eyes were sunken, with rings around them. Washing my face with cold water—which is an oxymoron in Florida, as the tap water is eighty degrees—did nothing for me. I brushed back my hair and tried to look a little more presentable. Taking a deep breath I went back into the lab.

"He's there and you can go over," Justine said.

I could tell something was up by her voice. "And?"

"Just be careful around him. You can't walk in there and tell him it's a murder when he's already ruled it an accidental death."

I got that. "Sure. Maybe I can just plant a seed of doubt."

"There you go, sow away," she said.

"Call you later?" I asked on my way out the door.

"You bet," she said, turning back to her work.

Her last words and the way she said them ran through my head on the drive to the medical examiner's office. It probably wasn't anything I should have been analyzing, but I had that "maybe-new-girlfriend, new-relationship" feeling that wouldn't let my brain drop it. I was in unfamiliar territory but was brought back to reality every few seconds by the nagging voice of Siri from my phone. After exiting the 836 at Northwest Twelfth Avenue, I worked my way around Jackson Memorial Hospital and found the Miami-Dade coroner's office. I had been there before but had never driven, making it a new experience.

I caught my second break when I found Sid at his desk instead of in the autopsy room. "Hey, Sid," I said, knocking on the doorjamb.

He peered at me over his glasses like I had done something wrong. "I hear you're looking into the Jane Doe from last night."

I wondered what Justine had told him. "I'm just trying to establish her identity now." I pulled my phone out and showed him the picture of her dive certification.

He pulled his glasses up on his balding head, swung a lighted magnifying glass over his desk, and studied the picture. "Bone structure's right. Could be her."

I explained about the gear and the tank. "If I could take a strand of her hair, Justine says she can try and match them."

"Done," he said, handing me a sealed evidence bag. "Make sure she's the one that opens it." He turned back to whatever he had been working on, essentially dismissing me.

This was going faster than I wanted it to. "I'm curious—"

He looked over his glasses again and cut me off. "She said this was your second case."

I expected that was bad. "It is. But there are some things bugging me."

He pushed his papers aside. "It's a slow night. Let's see what you got."

I took a deep breath, trying to control myself from blurting out everything. "Okay, I'm just going back to what you said." He gave me a look that said *continue*. "There was little bruising around the stomach area. You thought that was due to the time in the water and the internal organs being ripped out. I get that, and it brings me to the lung thing. There was something you noted about her lungs being overexpanded."

"That was curious, but she was definitely run over by a boat."

"I agree, but what would have made her lungs blow up, and could she have died from that before she was hit by the propeller?"

"We're assuming she was scuba diving when the accident occurred. That was unknown when we did the initial autopsy. Now that you found the gear it really doesn't change much. The cut straps on the BC still match the propeller theory. What I'm thinking is it was simultaneous. Kind of the opposite of drowning. If you were just swimming and were struck by a propeller, you would be alive, and your initial reaction, if you were disabled, would be to inhale a lungful of water. With scuba gear, it's the opposite. But it wouldn't expand the lungs, just keep water out."

That made sense. The obvious injury was the propeller and he was likely correct about the cause of death. But there was something still bugging me. I suspected neither of us knew enough about scuba to be certain about the lung expansion. That led me to the person who did.

"Once we establish the identity, I have to close the file." He paused. "Unless you can prove something else was the cause of death."

With the evidence bag in hand, I left his office thinking that the clock was ticking now, and although I was in control of the evidence that could confirm the victim's identity, I couldn't slow down the process. I sat in the Park Service truck with the windows open. It was past midnight now, and I wasn't sure what to do. I knew I was starting to freelance with the investigation and needed some time to think. Even though I didn't like him, I did have a boss to report to.

Before heading home, I needed to call Justine. There was no answer, so I left a voicemail saying I had to work early in the morning and would catch up with her tomorrow. I still had the hair sample, and with a somewhat clear conscience, I returned to the headquarters building. The drive that had taken over an hour earlier was less than half that now, and I pulled up behind the Park Service building and left the truck. Taking the keys with me, I headed toward the boat and hopped aboard, thinking I'd be back in the morning. Somehow I needed to square this investigation with Martinez before he figured out what I was doing.

The boat ride back was uneventful, and I surprised myself with another smooth docking maneuver. It was so stealthy that even Zero didn't hear me. I had thought that once my head hit the pillow, I would be asleep, but that was not the case. I tossed and turned for an hour before I decided to get up. This thing with Martinez was eating at me, and suspecting his reaction was not going to be in my favor, I wanted to see where I really stood.

I found the employee manual in the bottom of a neglected box deep in a closet. As with most things that involved paperwork, it was the first time the spine had been opened. Taking it to the living room, I sat on the couch and studied the table of contents. There were several sections that might contain what I was looking for and I flipped to the first one.

———

A LOUD CRACK OF THUNDER FOLLOWED CLOSELY BY A BRILLIANT stroke of lightning woke me. The lightning illuminated the room and was followed by another crash of thunder that shook the house. I had been warned, but I was still getting used to these daily storms. The weather out west was different. Cold fronts pushed through from mid-October through late March, bringing wind, rain, and snow. Once they stopped, the skies stayed clear until the next fall. In fact, there were weeks when you couldn't see a cloud and it often didn't rain from May to October. The temperature was different as well. Often reaching a hundred degrees, the afternoons and evenings could be uncomfortable, but each night it cooled down into the sixties.

Florida weather had been explained to me as seven months of summer and five months of hell. And this was the hell part. The thermometer hadn't dipped below eighty degrees since I had been there and though it rarely reached ninety, the humidity was suffocating. Thunderstorms, which had been only a once-or-twice-a-year occurrence back home, were a daily event during the hell months.

Wide awake now I picked up the open book that lay on my stomach and went to the kitchen. The clock said it was five after five. It would be daylight soon and I would have to deal with the world. After brewing a pot of coffee, I took a cup back to the couch, and this time sitting upright, I started reading the manual. I was into my second cup when, despite the caffeine, my vision started blurring from the government legalese. The first hint of daylight snuck through the sliding glass door, and fighting to keep my eyes open, I found what I was looking for.

Director's order number 9: *Park officers may conduct investigations (wherever that investigation may lead) of offenses against the United States committed in the national park system in the absence of investigation thereof by any other Federal law enforcement agency having investigative jurisdiction over the offense committed or with the concurrence of such other agency.*

By my reading, it was clear from that passage that I could pursue the investigation. Miami-Dade, for all their assistance and support, was not a federal agency and had not shown any interest in the investigation. The part that said "wherever it may lead" stated, at least to me, that I didn't have to stay in the confines of the park to work the case. I copied the section and page in a note on my phone and headed for the shower, feeling like I actually had a chance.

That feeling didn't last long. Standing in front of Martinez, two hours later, my confidence had waned and he hadn't even spoken yet. To make it worse, my phone had vibrated, showing a call from Justine, just after I had walked into his office. I would have liked to talk to her first.

"What the hell, Hunter?" he started.

This was not going at all the way I had planned.

"You find a body, then you go off the reservation and start an investigation?"

I knew he didn't want an answer, so I just let the train roll.

"Yes, I got your first complaint. Some guy asking what kind of authority you had to be pushing him around."

It had to be Gordy. I doubted Herb would remember or was even sober enough to call. It didn't matter. I had to make a stand sooner or later.

"I was trying to identify the victim," I started.

"Miami-Dade has the body. It's their job," he said.

I had to call him on this now or I would be looking for another job. "Actually, it is within our mandate to conduct investigations, wherever they may lead." It sounded pretty good to me.

His face turned from brown to red, which was a stretch. "Don't quote that shit to me. I'm your boss. We have rules and budgets."

I knew that he knew that he was standing on shaky ground. From my experience, as soon as a government employee says the word "budget" as a reason for anything, you can assume they are out of arguments. The question was how to play him. I figured him for the ego-driven bureaucrat. Now was the time to test my theory, not barrage him with regulations he probably already knew.

"Solving this could look good for us. A little publicity could get us an increase in our budget. As the special agent in charge, you'll probably get a promotion or commendation too." That was all I had. Giving him half the credit for no work. He sat straighter in his chair and I knew I had him.

"Short leash, Hunter, and no more complaints. You've apparently done your homework and know the limits of your authority —don't push it."

I wanted out before he changed his mind. "Yes, sir," I said, forcing myself not to salute him. It wasn't the best deal, and I knew he'd be the one in front of the cameras if we found any answers. I didn't care. I had a case to solve.

"Just one thing, surfer boy. That schedule you gave me. That's still your job too."

11

STEVEN BECKER

A KURT HUNTER MYSTERY

BACKWATER BAY

I LEFT Martinez's office relieved. That is, until I ran into Susan McLeash. It was as if she was stalking me and I guessed it wasn't a coincidence when she cornered me before I could get down the stairs.

"Hear you got a case going." It was a statement, not a question.

"Just working on the identity of the floater we found the other day." I had a feeling she too was angling for a piece of the credit if we scored some media attention. I was well aware that she had felt scorned the last time when she was left out.

"Thinking it's a homicide?"

That was a question that led me to believe she wasn't sure what I had. "Just trying to notify the next of kin," I said, trying to get down the first step. *Run, run fast, run fast and don't look back* was at the forefront of my agenda. As a woman, she wasn't unattractive. I figured her for early forties, just the age where vain women start to get desperate. Her platinum-streaked hair was a little too perfect and her uniform blouse a little too tight. Her contrived appearance told me she was trouble, and someone happy to take credit for my work.

Mariposa must have noticed and called my name as if she were going to scold me for something. In the pecking order of the head-quarters staff, the Jamaican woman had some kind of maternal power, and Susan backed away enough for me to slide downstairs. On my way out, Mariposa tried again to corral me into a dinner invitation. I carefully dodged her request as best I could until she finally gave me that look and I promised to ask Justine.

Procrastination, at least when it came to social engagements, was in my DNA, and I put the dinner from my mind. I had gained some traction with Martinez, but the reprieve from him would likely be short-lived. This brought me back to my top priority, now that the victim had a name: establishing the cause of death as a homicide. To do that I needed a quick education on scuba equip-ment. T. J. down in Key Largo would surely help. Through Justine, I had met him on my first case here.

Despite the early hour, the heat and humidity were building quickly. Sitting in the truck with the air conditioner running, I dialed Justine.

"He actually gave it to you?" she asked after I told her about Sid giving me the hair sample.

"You sound surprised."

"He's just not the trusting type. Maybe he likes you."

I didn't really know where to go with that, so I let it drop. "Any-way, I have the hair sample and a short leash from Martinez. There's some dive stuff I need help with too. Do you think you could hook me up with T. J.?"

There was a pause on the line and I wondered what I had done wrong now.

"There's also this propeller thing. Maybe he could help me with that too."

"You're talking homicide again?"

I had her attention. "Yeah, but I have to prove it to Sid before we confirm the identity. As long as she's a Jane Doe and he has some space, he's going to hold on to the body." My phone vibrated and I glanced down at it. The 305 area code told me it was from Miami; the caller ID was blank. "Hey, I gotta call you back."

I swapped calls. "Hello, this is Agent Hunter."

"You left your card with me last night."

I didn't have to ask the name. I had only handed out two cards and one was to a man. "Holly?"

"Yes. Can you come over?"

"What about Herb? I don't think he's going to be happy to see me."

"He's gone. Playing golf, or so he says. Probably be out for a while."

There was something about the way she said *gone* that spooked me. "Can we do this over the phone?"

"I would feel more comfortable in person."

It wasn't like I had a plan. "I can swing by in a half hour." I pulled out of the Park Service lot and redialed Justine.

"I have to go see Abbey's aunt. She says she has some information."

"That'll work if you want to bring the hair sample by afterward. I have a swing shift today from noon to eight."

The only problem with that was the identity of the body would be confirmed sooner than I wanted. I had to move fast. On my way up to the Gables, I wondered what information Holly could have that was so important she had to deliver it in person. By the time I realized that I couldn't think of anything, I was sitting in her driveway. Things looked worse in the daylight, and as I walked up the path I noticed the exterior of the house and landscape had been as poorly done as the interior. In my opinion, the dollars they had put into the house would never be recouped. The sunlight was not being kind to the property, and when I opened the door, I thought the same about the owner.

Holly stood in the doorway. She gave me a smile that almost

cracked her makeup. In a bright sundress that had seen better years, she stood trying to look alluring with her hand on her hip. Her other hand held a cup of coffee. Looking at her I had a quick image of Susan McLeash a few years from now. She invited me in, and I caught a whiff of the cup and almost choked. Straight vodka at ten thirty a.m. A little early for me, but it might have been late for her. She had made an attempt to look good, but it was hard to hide the dark circles under her eyes; it looked like she had been up all night.

"Would you like to sit down? Coffee?"

Wondering if the coffee was going to be the same as hers, I declined. "I'm good," I said, following her into the living room. She swayed slightly before she finally found the couch and sat closer to me than I thought necessary. "What can I do for you, ma'am?"

"It's Herb."

I'd had a feeling that was coming but didn't know how it was going to play out. I gave her a sympathetic nod.

"Well, you saw him. Man's a mess."

I couldn't argue that point, but it appeared to be a case of the pot calling the kettle black. I stayed silent, hoping she would open up.

"I know. Look at me. I've been up all night. He left just after you did. Took one of those Uber things."

"Is that unusual? He seemed under the influence."

"Neither—under the influence or unusual—but he's not real bright. I get the receipts sent to my email."

I was guessing that she knew where he had gone. "And . . ."

She deftly changed the subject. "I thought that might have been a bad first impression we gave you last night."

It wasn't the line of questioning I wanted to follow, but if she was talking, I was ready to listen. I'd found when dealing with scared people that saying nothing would get the other person talking—they hated dead air.

"The house, Abbey's apartment. Everything's a wreck. It's not like we abused her or anything. Things are hard now."

From the date of birth on Abbey's certification card, I knew she was twenty-five. Abuse was not an issue. She could have left whenever she wanted. Holly sidled closer to me. I was getting freaked out and slid just far enough away to avoid a confrontation and keep her talking. I must have put her off.

"This is all so hard." She took a deep drink from her mug.

I thought so too and wondered if I was here to provide comfort or solve a crime. "Mind if I have another look out back?" I asked.

"Not at all. I'll be right here," she said, hoisting the mug to her lips.

Holly was not going to be any more use, at least today. I left her in the living room and went down the small hallway, through the laundry, and outside. I tried not to judge the shoddy landscaping as I walked down the path to the small apartment. The door was ajar, and not trusting Holly that Herb was not there, I pulled out my gun and slowly pushed the door open with my shoe. The main room with the kitchen and living area was clear and I eased into the hallway. A quick glance confirmed the bathroom was empty. I found myself staring at the closed bedroom door.

I tapped it lightly with the tip of the barrel and, when there was no answer, walked in. Feeling a little stupid and hoping there were no video cameras, I started my investigation. Someone had made a half-hearted attempt to clean up the place since I had seen it last night. The furniture had been set back in place. Drawers were stuffed to overflowing and random things were still left on the floor; it looked like whoever had done it was trying to ease their guilt. There was no telling how the contents had been shuffled around, and forensic evidence would be worthless.

While I looked at her belongings that were sticking out of the drawers or still scattered on the floor and furniture, I observed two things in particular. I wondered about the quantity and quality of her stuff, and the reason this apparent crime had not been reported. This was a curious business. I wondered what whoever had done this had been after and why. I got the impression that Holly didn't leave the house much. Her concerns and anger issues with Herb, gave me the feeling that she was trying to say it was him without using the words. That might explain why there was no police report.

Twenty-something women had stuff. Clippings, pictures, cactus gardens. They were still young enough to hold on to their teenage years. Abbey had a lot of stuff, and I recognized some of the brands; they weren't from Target. It was apparent she had been making good money and I thought again about Gordy's business plan. Moving from her personal belongings, I started looking at the pictures, many pinned to the wall with thumbtacks and not framed. There were several from her high school years with friends and what looked like family. I saw a woman who bore a striking resemblance to Holly, presumably Abbey's mother. Another picture showed Abbey, Holly, and the same woman sitting side by side, suited up and ready to jump off a dive boat. Feeling dirty, I finished and left the door as I had found it and went back to the house.

The house felt empty, and I called out to Holly. There was no answer after several attempts and I had to decide if her condition might be life-threatening.

Considering the state she was in and the last two gulps of vodka I'd seen her take, I thought I'd better have a look around. It didn't take much investigative skill to find her curled up in a ball on the couch. I checked to make sure she was still breathing, put a blanket over her, and left the house. If there was something to be learned from her, it wasn't going to come out today.

———

JUSTINE WAS HUNCHED OVER A MICROSCOPE COMPARING SHELL casings. "Be just a few minutes," she said.

"Can I use a computer?"

"Sure, any of the ones on the counter are fair game."

Three computers were lined up on a table against a wall. I went to the far one and started hunting. There was something I couldn't understand about Abbey's being killed by a propeller wound to the stomach. If that was indeed the cause of death, she would have had to be floating on her back with her scuba gear on. Two possible scenarios came to mind. The first was that she was cleaning the bottom of a boat, and while she was near the stern, the engine started and was put into gear. I closed my eyes for a minute and tried to picture this. The second was that she was already dead and with the buoyancy of the wetsuit and BC was floating face up on the surface. Both brought up more questions than they answered.

Justine came over and looked at the pictures on the monitor. "Nice," she said, and pecked my cheek.

"That stomach-wound thing is bugging me."

"Most of these are hand and foot wounds," she said, looking at the screen.

"Exactly. She would have had to be cleaning the bottom of the boat when it was started and put in gear."

"Or already dead. She would have heard the engine start and freaked out. You can hear really well underwater. Not necessarily direction, but the engine starting would have been loud and clear."

"Makes you wonder how she got into the mangroves too."

"I want to have a look at the last boat she was working on. My friend Gordy gave me a name."

"Why don't you see about the boat, and I'll run the hair? Compare notes at dinner?"

We made plans to meet when she got off at eight. With a smile, I went back to my car. I had kept a weather eye on the storm clouds building since early morning and was rewarded when the skies opened with a brief but intense afternoon thunderstorm. The torrential rain slowed traffic to a crawl and the visibility was bad enough to cause many drivers to pull onto the shoulder to wait out the storm. I plowed ahead, thinking about my new BFF, Gordy.

With the palm of my hand, I rubbed the interior of the windshield, trying to help the defroster, and couldn't help but notice the fog coming out of the vent. Another Florida first. As suddenly as it had started the storm abated and the sun came out. With it, the traffic began moving again, and I reached the marina a few minutes before five. I parked and walked down the dock to the small building that held Bottoms Up's office. The air-conditioning was working overtime; the dripping condensation had made a deep indentation into the wood plank beneath it. I went around to the front and pulled on the sliding glass door handle, only to find it was locked.

"Hey, man, you looking for Gordon?" The fuel attendant asked.

I was wrong. He went by Gordon. "Yeah. National Park Service, I have some questions." That sounded lame. I thought about using *special agent*, but that was worse.

"Hangs out at the bar over there." He pointed to an outdoor bar near a long rectangular pool.

I thanked him, walked back to solid land, crossed the parking lot, and entered the pool area through a custom metal gate. The pool and deck were empty. It looked like the storm had driven everyone to the bar. I walked up and stood on my tiptoes to see if I could find old Biff. I heard him before I saw him. Before I confronted him again, I wanted to get a sense of the lay of the land.

I felt a little like a creeper standing behind a large potted palm tree and spying on Gordy, but in my capacity as a special agent, it was called investigative work and part of the job. That made me feel a little better. He sat in the shade at the bar under large rotating fans, with a cool drink in his hand, while I baked on the pool deck. He had a woman on either side of him and appeared to be holding court.

It seemed like a pretty comfortable scene until I looked at the faces of the people sitting around the bar. The only word that came to mind was *losers*. The men had comb-overs and potbellies, the women too much makeup and too few clothes. It was also a little early, in my opinion, for the amount of alcohol being consumed. From a quick scan of the drinks sitting on the bar, I determined these were not froufrou cocktails from a laminated menu with parrots on it. These folks were drinking straight alcohol. There was nothing to be gained here, and I looked out at the marina, wondering where the *Big Bang* was docked.

Beads of sweat dripped from my forehead. It was hotter than ten hells. It's an interesting phenomenon in South Florida that despite what the thermometer says, it seems hotter after it rains. The temperature will usually drop about ten degrees—from nine to seven on my hell scale—but the humidity jumps to a hundred percent.

I couldn't put it off any longer and walked over to the bar. "Hello, Gordon," I said, watching his reaction carefully. I didn't need my trained observation skills to notice when he gagged on his drink. "Just a few questions." I cocked my head over toward a quiet corner. He said something to a woman sitting next to him. Even through her heavy makeup, she looked familiar, and I did a double take. Gordy ignored me and we moved to a quiet corner of the bar.

"I have a question," I said.

"Go ahead. I'm a little busy."

I caught his glance over to the woman. I figured I'd make it simple. "Who ordered the work on the *Big Bang* and where is it docked?"

He looked back to the bar. Another man had taken his seat and was talking up the woman. I saw his glance and caught a break. There was a hesitation, as if he were calculating whether I would find out without him. He clammed up, and I tried a different tack. "That woman looks familiar," I said, turning in the direction of the woman he had been with at the bar. She was gone and I saw a confused look on his face. Watching his gaze shift to the docks, I saw her following a man who seemed to be ignoring her. When they were out of sight, he turned back to me.

"Brenda. She owns the *Big Bang*."

STEVEN BECKER

A KURT HUNTER MYSTERY

BACKWATER BAY

NOT SURE IF the moisture pouring from my skin was sweat or if it was the cloud I was walking through, I headed over to the dockmaster's office and asked where I might find the *Big Bang*. Before I talked to the owner, I wanted to see what I was dealing with. The dockmaster took one look at my uniform and pointed me in the direction of a large yacht.

Passing a line of fishing charters and sailboats, I entered the high-rent district of the marina, and though I knew little about boats, I could see most of these were sixty feet plus. They were two- and three-stories high, their upper decks and towers looming over me. Stainless steel gleamed and polished teak glistened as I inspected each boat. It was quiet on the dock. The boaters who were actually in residence had taken cover in their air-conditioned salons and there were only a few maintenance workers out.

I reached the *Big Bang*. She was every bit of sixty feet and the shadow of her three decks covered the dock. I walked past her, trying to do an inspection, although I wasn't sure what I was looking for—or at. Basic boat nomenclature was fairly simple, and I had mastered *port*, *starboard*, *bow*, and *stern* as well as the other basics. After reaching the bow, I studied the waterline on the walk back to the stern. Nothing struck me as unusual, but it probably wouldn't. These people had hired help for everything: cleaning bottoms, cleaning decks, cooking, and whatever other jobs were needed aboard a boat this size. If there was some evidence here, it would have been removed weeks ago.

"Ahoy," I called out. It sounded goofy, but this is what you did. I added a more conventional greeting: "Anyone home?"

There was no answer, but I thought I saw the reflection of a TV in the smoked-glass window. I heard voices and called out again, rapping my fist against the gunwale like it was a door knocker. Still no answer. The voices raised, and I tensed when I heard a man and a woman. My instincts said domestic disturbance. I wasn't sure where the line was on interfering in a dispute or searching a vessel but decided that the deck was fair game. I was used to hopping down from the dock to the Park Service's center-console, but this ship needed a small set of three steps to reach its deck.

The white fiberglass sparkled from the beads of moisture that had not yet been baked off by the sun, making the deck look like a field of diamonds. The fight intensified to the point that I started worrying that it might get violent. I crossed the deck and knocked on the salon door. There was no answer. The voices were louder and clearer here. Then something smashed against a wall and the woman screamed. I tried to look inside, but the tinted glass did its job, dimming the interior of the cabin, and I moved closer, almost pressing my face to the door to see inside.

It was quiet now and I had to make a decision. From what I had already heard, I judged that I had cause, and opened the door. The first thing I saw was a man's body on the floor. Thinking I had reacted too late and had his blood on my hands, I knelt down next to him and felt for a pulse. It was weak but there. Slowly he regained his senses.

"Sir," I called out, probably louder than I should have.

"He's not deaf and he's not dead," the woman said.

I looked around, searching for the voice. My eyes had not yet adjusted from the blinding deck to the dim cabin and it took two passes before I saw the shape of a body on the settee. The man moved, and my attention was drawn back to him.

"Are you injured?" I asked.

He worked his way to his knees. "I'm lucky I'm not dead." Rising slowly, he brushed himself off.

I rose as well and we faced each other. He was a good three inches taller than my six feet and probably in better shape than I was. It was strange to look at him as a victim, but he was the one who had been assaulted. "Do you want to press charges?"

He looked over at the woman on the couch. "No, just get her off my boat."

"It's not yours until you pay me my half." She sounded bitter.

"Don't ever get married," he said, brushing past me.

Before I could react, he was out the door and I felt the boat rock slightly as he climbed onto the dock. There was not much I could do if he didn't want to press charges, and even if he did, I was out of my jurisdiction and I would have to call in Miami-Dade.

I turned back to the woman on the settee. She had clearly recovered from whatever had happened and sat with a smug look on her face. "Hello, ma'am. Kurt Hunter with the Park Service." I walked closer.

"Brenda," she said, extending a limp wrist. "I don't fish or anything."

I gave her hand a quick shake. It felt cold and clammy, and looking down on it, even in the dim light I could see sunspots and veins, standing proud on her skin. She was older than I had guessed, making her heavy makeup and skimpy "boating" clothes look out of place. Maybe a thirty or even a forty-something could pull off that look, but not her. After a quick study, I determined she was in her fifties. My vision had acclimated and I confirmed it was the same woman that Gordy had been sitting next to at the bar—the one who looked like Holly.

"We're the Park Service. Fish and Game handles that kind of thing." She sat there with a coy look on her face. I noticed her anger gone and her mood had taken a turn like a tarpon when it feels the hook.

"Then what can I do for you, Mr. Hunter?"

She drew out my name like she had been drinking. The man had left the salon door open and I looked down the dock to see if anyone had seen what happened. The heat had kept them all inside. "Mind if I ask you a few questions?"

"The man is Gabe Kniesel. He's still technically my husband. As you heard, the divorce isn't final yet."

"And I'm guessing the boat is standing in the way."

"He's supposed to pay me half the market value. Except he had a crooked surveyor lowball it. I should get what's due me. Don't you agree?"

I swear she winked at me when she said it. Not caring to offer an opinion on the state of her divorce, I asked what I had originally come to find out. "Did you have the bottom cleaned a few weeks ago?" I asked.

"Shithead takes care of the maintenance. I was traveling, so I wouldn't know."

It didn't take a trained investigator to know who she was talking about. "Really nice boat, mind if I look around?"

"I'd be happy to give you a tour." She smiled. With an effort she rose, staggered slightly, and sat back down. "The heat gets to me," she offered as an explanation.

I felt the boat shift and looked back through the open door to see Gordy stepping down the stairs to the deck.

"What's going on in there?" he asked as he walked into the salon.

"Brenda's okay," I said, hoping that was what he wanted to know. I saw the look he exchanged with Brenda and thought I might stick around for a while. Turning an investigative eye toward him, I decided to try to get some insight into what was going on here. "Her husband is okay too."

"That's good," he said.

He was glancing around, figuring out how to make his exit. I stood in his way, trying to make him uncomfortable. "Mind if I ask what brings you here?"

There was a long pause. Finally, he came up with an answer. "I'm trying to collect for the bottom cleaning and zinc replacement. I saw Gabe heading to the boat earlier."

"Did he pay you?" I asked, wanting to make a note of the zinc replacements. I had no idea what that meant and filed it away in my head; if I took the time to take out my pad and pen, the moment might be lost. It was also noteworthy that he'd called Gabe by his first name.

"Her ex is being a ballbuster and wanting to see the old zincs. He was all uptight about it."

Brenda started fidgeting on the couch. She shot him a conspiratorial look and I sensed there was nothing more to be gained by staying. Thanking them for their time, I left the salon, crossed the deck, and climbed the stairs to the dock. As I walked back toward my truck, I realized I was more confused now than when I started.

Before leaving the parking lot, I took out my notepad and wrote down what Gordy had said about the zincs as well as Gabe's name.

13

BACKWATER BAY

THE INCIDENT on the *Big Bang* had me in a tailspin. I hadn't figured on my floater putting me in the middle of a family soap opera. I had evidence building and suspects coming and going but, two days into my investigation, I had no confirmed identity and the cause of death was still a boating accident. It was close to six now. Martinez would be off work and at either the driving range or the bar. I worried about another complaint and knew if I could not confirm Abbey's identity and convince Sid this was a homicide, not an accident, I would be back on the flats of Biscayne Bay tomorrow morning. On most days, that would have been my preference, but I was getting invested in this case and wanted to see it through.

The dashboard clock read five forty-five when I pulled into traffic and headed toward the Miami-Dade crime lab. Traffic was light over the causeway and fifteen minutes later I pulled into the parking lot in front of Justine's office. I grabbed the evidence bag from the seat and with fat raindrops landing on my head, walked across the parking lot and into the building. As if on cue, a loud boom of thunder shook the glass door just as it closed. I looked back at the rain, now coming down in sheets and blocking the parking lot from view, and wondered if this was an indicator of how my visit would go.

Justine was at her desk and gave me a panicked look when I walked in. She motioned me to a chair in the next cubicle and held up a finger, signaling for me to wait. I saw the reason for her distress when I heard a detective's voice. Pushing the chair back as far as it would go, I lifted my legs and tried to be invisible, feeling for a minute like I was a kid hiding in a toilet stall.

"I'll be back for the forensics," he said. It was Dwayne's old partner. We had never proven that he was involved in the refugee case, but we hadn't disproved it either. My presence would definitely have been unwelcome.

I heard the door close and watched her go to the plate-glass window that looked out into the hallway to make sure he was gone. She came over and pecked me on the cheek.

I felt my blood rise and wanted to reach for her, but she moved away. I quickly rationalized that by deciding she was just being professional, ignoring me in case he came back.

"Let's have a look at that hair," she said, breaking the ice.

We were back to the easier working relationship. The personal one was on hold. I followed her to a stainless steel table.

She pulled on blue nitrile gloves and, using a pair of tweezers, removed the hair from the evidence bag. Taking one strand, she positioned it on a slide and slid it under the microscope. A second later, the image from the eyepiece appeared on the computer screen and she worked the mouse to focus and resize the window to take up half the display. From another bag, she took out the hair sample from the brush and I watched the monitor as the next image appeared.

Side by side, they looked identical to me. I now had enough experience in these matters to hold my tongue and wait for Justine to finish. It took less time than I expected; a minute later, she pronounced they were the same.

"I need to get DNA testing done to confirm, but they're a match."

We had cleared the first hurdle. "Can you let Sid know?"

"Sure, but how are you going to deal with a boating accident not being the cause of death?"

I'd been thinking about this and had a few ideas. My first thought had been trying to figure out how the incision the propeller had made in Abbey's stomach had occurred. This was problematic and even with my limited boating knowledge, if you wanted to run something over, the bow would hit the body, throwing it to one side or another and out of reach of the propeller. The boat would have had to back up to her. I remembered Sid saying that he thought the prop was running at a thousand rpms. That was pretty fast for reverse.

"What about that thing with her lungs."

"I read the transcript. He said there were burst blood vessels, like they had overinflated."

"Right. That couldn't have happened after death. If we can prove what caused it, we may have our cause of death."

Justine went to her desk and started typing. I watched over her shoulder as she did a search for "overinflated lungs." Three-quarters of the way down the search results page I got the feeling we were onto something. There was an article on the Divers Alert Network about pulmonary overinflation syndrome. She scrolled through the content faster than I could read it, forcing me to wait for her synopsis.

"Boyle's law states that the volume of a gas acts inversely to the pressure it is under. The more pressure applied, the more compressed the gas becomes. One of the first laws of scuba diving is to never hold your breath. This is especially dangerous on the ascent. When you breathe in and out, the lungs compensate for the changing pressure, but if you were to hold your breath, the volume of gas would expand as you rose through the water."

"That makes sense, except isn't it shallow in those canals?"

"Shallow water is actually more dangerous. The smaller the numbers the larger the percentage change."

"Okay, but she was an experienced diver."

Justine shrugged. "People do all kinds of stupid stuff when they dive."

I could believe that after some of the situations I had recently bailed boaters, hikers, and fishermen out of. Boyle's law might have explained the physics of what happened, but there had to be a human element as well.

"It could be equipment failure and still be an accidental death," she said.

I got the feeling she was getting worn out by my persistence. I knew she was already busy. Maybe I was pushing her too hard to back me up. I didn't believe this was an accidental death, especially after meeting the cast of characters involved. I was sure one of them had killed her. Before I could fill her in on what had happened that afternoon, the door opened and a pair of detectives walked in. I ducked into a corner to avoid them. They approached Justine's desk.

"Hey, Doey," one of the men said.

The nickname didn't seem to bother her. It was likely just some police-brotherhood thing. Maybe I had been on the politically correct West Coast for too long. "Doey" sounded demeaning to me. Catching myself before I did anything stupid, I looked around the corner of the cubicle and tried to observe their interaction impartially.

The guy might have been a wise-ass, but there was no hint of the tension I had seen between her and Dwayne, the bad cop we had taken down several weeks ago. Before they could reach her desk, she rose and led them to a stainless steel table that held several evidence boxes. I caught her eye as she talked to the men and waited while she steered them around the table so they had their backs to me. I made a motion with my hand indicating that I would call her later and slid toward the door.

One of the men must have heard me and started to turn, but Justine took something out of one of the boxes and started talking. It distracted him enough for me to make a clean escape. It wasn't lost on me that I was escaping from a police lab, but I didn't want to endanger Justine's position by being there.

Once I was out of the building, I moved to the side of the entrance and caught my breath. Thinking about the time and knowing that Martinez would be all over me for a report on my schedule, I decided to head back to Homestead and my house on Adams Key.

Something nagged at me as I pulled out of the lot and wove my way toward the Palmetto Expressway. On the highway I saw the exit for the 836 and, without thinking, turned onto the eastbound ramp and headed to the beach. I didn't know if the dive shop would be open this late but decided the short detour was worth the risk. I had thought about taking the trip down to Key Largo to see T. J., but that was going to be a four-hour round trip, plus whatever time I spent there. I didn't have the better part of a day.

Fifteen minutes later, I was over the causeway and turned right onto Alton Road. I pulled into the marina and parked near the building where the dive shop was located. As I got out of the car, I noticed the lights were on in the store. I reached the door only to find it locked and walked over to the window, where I could see inside. There were three rows of chairs set up with their backs toward me. I quickly counted a dozen people. The man who had identified Abbey stood in front of them writing on a whiteboard.

I waited until he seemed to pause and knocked on the glass. After shooting me an annoyed look, he came to the door. Sometimes my uniform has its advantages and a few minutes later, I was sitting in the back row of the makeshift classroom. I had gotten a reluctant agreement to talk, but he was adamant about finishing his class. After listening for a few minutes, I guessed this was the first class in the open water certification course, a deduction I was able to make by sneaking a look at the book in the lap of the man next to me.

"And the first rule of diving is to never hold your breath," the instructor said, pointing at the words on the board as he spoke them.

He had my attention now and I listened intently as he reviewed the basics of diving. When I glanced at my watch I saw it was already nine o'clock. What I had thought was fifteen minutes had been close to an hour. I looked back up and saw he was assigning homework. The class broke up and I waited patiently while he spent time answering the students' questions. It was a mixed bag of people: a father and daughter, two middle-aged women, a group of thirty-somethings, and a few scattered men. After he finished with the last question and said goodbye to the students, I approached.

"Well, Detective, ready to learn to scuba?"

I decided that *detective* was a little less pretentious than *special agent* and let it go. "Actually yes, but that's not why I'm here." I could see him shut down and cursed myself for my bedside manner. "Some diving questions really," I said, trying to climb out of the hole I had dug.

"Sure thing. Any luck with Abbey?"

"That's why I'm here. Was she a good diver?"

He paused for a minute, thinking about how to answer the question. "*Good diver* is a relative term. There are all kinds of divers and types of dives. She was good at what she did, but I have no idea how she was in open water."

I nodded. All I had wanted to know was that she wasn't a rookie. "I heard you talking about not holding your breath when you're diving. Would that apply in shallow water, like when she was cleaning a boat bottom?" I ran my theory past him.

He thought for a minute. "I'd think it doubtful. I've moon-lighted and cleaned my share of hulls. It's harder than you'd think, but the maximum draft of most boats is less than ten feet."

It was my turn to pause. He bailed me out. "If you tell me what you found, I may be able to piece it together."

"Overinflation of the lungs."

"Really? That's exactly what happens when you hold your breath at depth and ascend, but I can't see it happening from ten feet or less."

"Any other ideas?"

He walked toward a rack of gear and lifted what I guessed was a regulator from a display. "These have been known to jam and can free-flow, but she was pretty good about getting her gear serviced."

I took the mouthpiece from him and turned it in my hand. It was evident how it worked. "Couldn't she just spit it out?"

"You'd think so, but strange things happen underwater."

It wasn't hard to imagine what he was talking about and I had the image of a hand holding the mouthpiece in place. "Is there a way to make it . . ." I paused, trying to remember the words. "Free flow?"

He took the regulator and went toward the back room. I followed him to the tank-filling station, where he took a tank and screwed the fitting on the regulator to the valve. "This is the first stage and controls the pressure going to the hoses." He showed me the high-pressure line feeding the gauges and the low-pressure hose with a quick disconnect that supplied air to the buoyancy compensator. "These are both regulators. One's a primary and the other we call an octopus, which is used to supply emergency air to another diver."

"She didn't have one of those."

"I wouldn't expect her to. Cleaning hulls you usually dive alone, and the extra gear is just something else to get in the way."

He turned on the tank valve, picked up the primary regulator, and pushed a round button set on its face. Air rushed out of the mouthpiece. I was surprised at the force and set my hand by the outlet to feel the flow. It seemed that if this were stuck in your mouth, it could do the damage Sid had pointed out.

"That answer your question?"

"It does." I thanked him and left the store, thinking I had found the real cause of death and there was indeed foul play involved. Now I needed a motive.

14

STEVEN BECKER

A KURT HUNTER MYSTERY

BACKWATER
BAY

WALKING out of the dive shop, I noticed the storefront next door. Pictures of all kinds of boats for sale plastered the windows, and I scanned the listings. The divorce thing had me curious about how much the *Big Bang* was worth. Maybe putting a dollar value on it would justify the backstabbing I had witnessed, or even the death of a young woman, though I doubted it. As I moved closer to the door, the boats turned from smaller vessels to yachts, and the prices went from five figures to six and then seven. It was in the latter price range that I found the *Big Bang*. The Selene 60 was listed at 1.8 million dollars. It wasn't worth a dead body but sure explained a lot. Plenty of people have been killed for a lot less.

I walked past the bar on the way to the parking lot and wasn't the least bit surprised when I saw my favorite couple sitting together. In fact, not much had changed since that afternoon except the bartender. I stood off to the side by a stuccoed column thinking I was out of sight. As it turns out, a uniform is a magnet, and before I could react, I saw Brenda's eyes locked on to me. I thought about making a run for it. That plan had no legs and mine started to tremble as she sauntered toward me.

There wasn't even the remote possibility that she was heading anywhere else. Despite a slight sway, she was moving on an intercept path with my position. She clearly hadn't sobered up since our earlier introduction, which was the reason I didn't want an encounter now.

I'd had a bouncer's lifetime's worth of dealing with people on drugs and alcohol out west. You would think a beautiful remote wilderness would be overrun with Sierra Club–card-carrying do-gooders. My experience proved otherwise. There were the random hikers and fly fishermen, but the forest was full of people up to no good. Miners, pot growers, and poachers all seemed to get their courage from drugs and alcohol. An encounter with an inebriated person was inherently risky and the woman approaching me was no different.

"My favorite officer," she cooed.

I instinctively took a step back, trying to anticipate her next move. It almost put me out of her reach, but when she tripped and fell forward, whether by accident or design, I found her in my arms. When she looked up at me, I knew I had been played. I tried to lean her against the column and escape her grasp, only to find her falling into me again, this time using her breasts to cushion the blow.

"Brenda," I started, trying to remember her last name. "Maybe you should go back to your boat and sleep it off."

"Maybe you should walk me back."

I looked back toward the bar and saw Gordy watching us. Her invitation had one purpose for her and another for me, and I weighed the potential gain versus the risk. She had started to give me a tour of the boat earlier, only we were interrupted. This might be a chance to have a look without the inconvenience of a search warrant. After all, if I was invited aboard, there should be no repercussions. Her next move warned me of the risk, and I backed away. Before I could escape, she was on me again, pressing all her assets into me. Surprisingly it was Gordy who saved me.

"A few drinks and she gets the Brenda Braves. I'll take it from here," he said, grabbing her around the waist and leading her away. Suddenly, she crumpled like a rag doll. He looked at me and I knew I wasn't done. "A little help?"

There was nothing I could do but provide assistance. Together we half carried, half dragged Brenda to the boat. I was close to suggesting we use one of the wheelbarrows. It took both of us to haul her dead weight over the gunwales. Once aboard, we dumped her on the couch in the salon and stood looking at each other.

"Anything new about Abbey?" he asked.

I looked around the salon. It wasn't how I had planned on getting in, but I was there and didn't want to squander the chance. "It's being ruled an accidental death," I said. It was the truth until I could get to Sid with the information I had just learned at the dive shop. I studied his face as I said it. There was no indication that he was relieved or surprised.

"This can be a dangerous business. Working underwater in a busy marina. Sometimes, they forget you're there."

I remembered the A-frame signs in his office warning that Bottoms Up Boat Cleaning was at work. "Don't the signs help?"

"People are idiots. There's a lot of alcohol running around these places too," he said, looking over at Brenda on the couch.

"How's business?" I wanted to draw him out about his own financial situation.

"Summer in Miami, I'm surprised anyone's even here. Look around. At least half these yachts won't see their owners until December."

"Must be bad for business."

"Not really. You know what they say about boats: a hole in the water that you throw money into. Unless they haul them out, they need their bottoms cleaned at least twice a year. Paying one of my ladies is a whole lot cheaper than dry dock."

"So, it's usually the captain that schedules the maintenance and hires you?"

"On the big boys, yes. Some of the smaller boats, the owner takes care of maintenance themselves. Charter captains are good customers as well. We try and steer clear of the sailboats though. Keels are hell to clean, and the owners are tightwads."

"Who booked the cleaning for this boat?"

"Gabe takes care of everything. I'm not sure why Brenda's showing such an interest in it."

I thought he had something to say and waited, keeping my mouth closed, knowing people had a tendency to keep talking to fill a void. He was already on a roll. Unfortunately, it didn't work.

"If that's all, it's been a long one."

He was hiding something, but it could have just as easily been unreported income as something to do with Abbey's death.

Surprisingly he went to the door and opened it. I was sure he was going to wait for me to leave first, but he stepped out and a minute later I felt the boat shift when he climbed onto the dock. I watched him walk down the dock until he was out of sight. Brenda appeared to be asleep on the settee, leaving me essentially alone. Reviewing the laws on searches, I deemed that I had been invited aboard and a quick look around was entirely legal.

I had tried to watch Justine work with an unbiased eye and, knowing she was thorough, attempted to work as she would have. Not expecting to find forensic evidence, I wasn't worried about gloves and documenting every step I took. Looking around, I doubted there was much to be learned in the salon. Instead I decided to search the rest of the boat. Forward and to port was a stairway that went down to the staterooms. To starboard was a passage to the galley and helm. I decided to start with the galley and helm. I entered the small passage and found myself in a well-appointed kitchen. Rich wood cabinets adorned the walls of a fully-equipped galley. There was nothing to differentiate this from the kitchen in a custom home. Opening the side-by-side refrigerator, I found everything fully stocked. Forward was a settee with a large window looking out over the foredeck and bow.

I worked my way back to the main salon. Brenda lay where I had left her and I moved up a short flight of stairs to the bridge. What I had expected and what I was looking at were very different. The starship *Enterprise* had fewer electronics than the array set into the polished walnut dashboard. The helm was unusual. Equipped with several joysticks, it looked more like a video game controller than a ship's helm.

With nothing to show for my efforts, I backtracked to the port-side stairway and descended to the lower deck. I found two smaller staterooms, both empty. A closed door at the end of the hall beckoned. Opening it, I found myself in a richly-appointed master bedroom suite. Brenda appeared to have taken ownership. Clothes were all over the floor, looking like they had been brushed off the bed. An unmade bed tells a story, and from looking at this one, it was clear that two people had occupied it recently. There were indentations in both pillows and I could tell by the way the sheets lay that it had been exited from both sides. Brenda had had company recently.

A quick search of the drawers showed little, only confirming her taste in skimpy clothing. You could have laid out what looked like a dozen of her bathing suits to form a quilt that wouldn't have covered a small child. The suite had its own head, which had too much makeup on the counter and two towels on the tile floor.

The closet door was slightly ajar, and I pulled it open. It looked like the dumping ground for everything the previous occupant—a man, judging by the clothing—had left behind. I kicked the pile and my foot struck something. Leaning over, I delicately moved aside a pile of clothes that may have been clean or dirty; I couldn't tell. A heavy-duty case sat on the floor.

It looked like it was made to protect something, and from the orange color and scuff marks, not something you would expect to find in the master stateroom closet. I pulled it out and set it on the bed. Staring at the heavy-duty clasps, I paused, and after hearing no movement from Brenda, I opened it. Inside were a dozen different-size pieces that looked similar to the one I had found in the pocket of Abbey's BC. I picked one up and rubbed my hand against the smooth surface, remembering the stone-like texture of the one Abbey had.

One thing I had learned about boats was that they telegraphed even the smallest movement. When the deck shifted twice I suspected I had company. The movement settled, and I heard voices now. The legality of my invitation aboard might be in question if anyone found Brenda passed out on the couch and a uniformed agent in her bedroom.

Trying to figure out a graceful exit, I closed the case and set it back in the closet. After quickly tossing clothes over it, I turned and realized I still had the piece in my hand. I stood motionless for a minute, staring into the closet and trying to figure out what to do. I may have been there legally, but that didn't give me the right to take evidence. It was quiet now. Whoever had been moving around had stopped. When I turned around, Brenda stood in the doorway.

"Anything I can help you with?"

There was nothing I could say to justify my being there. I slipped the piece into my pocket, knowing the next move was hers. I suspected I knew what it might be. Being caught in the lair of a wealthy lush was not on my bucket list and I quickly searched for a way out. She moved closer and her hand reached for the top button on her blouse. It was so low-cut there were only five. She was through the third already and within inches of my face when the boat moved.

It caught her off guard too, and when the boat shifted again, she lost her balance and fell into me. At least this time I knew it wasn't an act, and I caught her, guiding her to the bed. She reached for me, trying to pull me onto her, but the boat moved again. Using the movement to my advantage, I rolled off her and gained my feet.

"I better see what's going on," I said, sliding through the doorway.

STEVEN BECKER

A KURT HUNTER MYSTERY

BACKWATER BAY

I HAD GAINED the deck and saw the cause of the movement. A boat sped past an adjacent dock, kicking up a large wake behind it. Other boaters were on their decks now, yelling at the driver to slow down. Relieved both that it had saved me from the temptress and that there was no one else aboard, I paused by the gunwale. The light behind me shifted and I saw a shadow.

Brenda was standing in the doorway. Something about her had changed. I had seen this look before and it was never good. Her eyes, only minutes ago had looked soft and seductive, now they were like orbs of stone. She was mad and coming straight for me. I had no idea where the anger was coming from, if she had seen me searching her cabin or if it was because I'd rebuffed her advances. Fortunately, she was slight. Maybe five-two and a little over a hundred and ten pounds, soaking wet.

She took a swing at me, but I caught her fist with my hand and gently turned her away, easing her toward the transom. The fire quickly died and I wondered what was going on.

"Men don't say no to me," she sobbed.

At least now I knew what it was. Before I could respond the

yacht bumped against the dock again and I saw my chance for escape. Brenda sat on the deck and offered no resistance as I jumped onto the transom and hopped across the two feet of water to the dock. I glanced back and saw Brenda peering over the gunwale.

I felt sorry for her and realized that since I'd turned her away so easily, there was no way she could have subdued Abbey, who was four or five inches taller and outweighed her by twenty pounds. Abbey was also experienced in the water. It was someone stronger who had killed her.

I waited until I was well down the dock before taking my phone out and dialing Justine's number. She answered on the second ring. "I got something I need you to look at."

"Hey to you too."

"Hey, sorry." I caught her up on the last few hours.

"Send me a picture and I'll see what I can do. Right now, I have those two dicks hanging around waiting for me to process their case."

"I will." I didn't want the conversation to end this way. "I gotta keep Martinez happy and do some patrol tomorrow. How about we catch up tomorrow night?"

"That'd be good."

I disconnected, wondering how long I could keep doing double duty before it caught up to me. I was more confused now than I had been that morning, and with Justine tied up and nowhere else to turn right now I looked forward to some sleep. The bar was on my way to the parking lot and I glanced over. Gordy was there holding court between two new women. I'd had enough of this crew for the day and moved to the shadows to avoid being seen.

Back at the truck, I pulled the plate I had found from my pocket, set it on the seat, and took a picture. I sent that with a text message to Justine and headed back to Homestead. Half an hour later, I reached the headquarters building with nothing solved. After leaving the truck in the back parking area, I walked to my boat, and realized just how tired I was.

———

IT HAD BEEN AN EASY RIDE ACROSS THE BAY AND I MANAGED TO DOCK against a flood tide without waking Zero—a sure measure of success. Despite how tired I felt, my mind churned away and I had a hard time sleeping. Finally I fell asleep only to find myself feeling groggy and sluggish. The sun was just up and I doubted I'd had more than three or four hours of good sleep. Two cups of coffee solved that problem and I headed out to the dock. Zero found me this time and, with his body firmly between me and the boat, rubbed against my leg while I scratched his ears.

"Gotta go, my friend," I told him, pushing him aside with my leg. Grabbing the bowline, I hopped down to the center-console and started the engine. There was no wind and little current, allowing the boat to sit in place as I released the stern line and pushed away from the dock. Proud of my last two docking maneuvers, I put the boat in gear and set a course for the pair of towers that marked the Turkey Point power plant, where the schedule I had given Martinez said I would be. The two chimneys were one of those unique things about Biscayne Park, and I found it ironic that in the middle of an iconic wilderness preserve stood a nuclear power plant.

Today was one of those rare days where the water looked more like a lake than an ocean. Running at twenty knots with the wind rushing through my hair cleared the last of the cobwebs from my head and things started to fall into place.

I thought I knew how Abbey had been killed, but the motive eluded me. I suspected it was money, and that it likely had something to do with the fight between Brenda and Gabe. Brenda came off as a victim, and unless she was much stronger and craftier than I gave her credit for, she was not the killer. Gabe was protecting what was his baby and probably the only asset Brenda's lawyer hadn't taken from him. I doubted he would have anything to do with a crime aboard. That could tie the boat up as a crime scene or it could even be confiscated. If he had done it, I guessed it would have been elsewhere. For the rest of them, I didn't like Gordy, but that didn't make him guilty of anything besides being an ass. He was arrogant and crafty, a deadly combination, but Abbey had worked for him and people don't often kill off their revenue streams. Herb and Holly were involved somehow. There was every indication that they were in financial trouble, but I couldn't figure their angle for killing Abbey. Alibis were another problem. They were useful in solving many crimes, but Abbey's death had a window of almost two weeks.

I was caught in a bad spot and my confidence started to wane. If Abbey was killed while cleaning the bottom of the *Big Bang* in the marina it was really Miami-Dade's case and I would have to give it up. If the body had been run over by a boat, it was an accidental death and I had no reason to investigate it.

It was then that the missing link came to me. How did the body get from the marina in South Beach to the mangroves in the backwaters of Biscayne Bay? There were only two ways I knew for the body to travel that distance. One was by boat and the other by water, and I wondered if a strong outgoing tide was powerful enough to relocate the body.

I had learned to read moving water; the eddies and currents in the streams out west were generally easy to see. The tidal currents here and the effect of the wind on them were different. Slowing down to an idle, I coasted to the shoreline, pulled my phone out, and opened one of the apps I had loaded that showed the wind and tides. I had learned to read the graph over the last month and understood some tides were more powerful than others, especially around the full and new moons. I would have to check the date range later, but for now, there was a fairly strong outgoing tide. The tidal range gave an indication of the speed of the current. The larger the swing, the more water had to move between low and high tide. With the current phase of the moon, the five-foot swing meant the water would be moving fast.

Lacking a body, I looked through the holds on the boat, finally settling on a fender. After tying a line to it, I tossed it overboard and watched. Wearing a wetsuit, Abbey was probably buoyant enough to float at or near the surface, something the propeller tearing through her would back up. I watched the buoy drift toward the barrier islands at a surprising rate. It took less than a minute to take out the entire hundred feet of line. When it came taut, a visible wake continued to pull at it.

The math was fuzzy, but I had nothing better to do with Martinez probably glued to his computer screen watching my movements. To support this theory, the VHF radio went off, startling me to the point that I almost dropped my phone overboard. I gave him my position and told him I had found an abandoned trapline—something that wouldn't require an incident report but was a hazard to navigation and would need to be removed from the water. Even over the crackle of static on the radio, the disappointment in his voice that I was actually doing my job according to the schedule I had submitted was evident.

Back to work now, I pulled in the line and opened the stopwatch app on my phone. Just behind the transom, I dropped the buoy in the water and tossed over the coiled line behind it. Seconds started to tick off and I waited patiently for the line to reach its limit. When it did, I stopped the timer and saw it had taken just thirty seconds for the buoy to reach the extent of the hundred-foot line. Taking the two numbers together, the hundred feet of distance and time equated to over two miles an hour. If the tides were about the same at the time she was killed, even with no wind, it would have taken about three or four hours for the body to float across the bay before it was trapped in the mangroves.

Sitting on the gunwale, I scrolled back to July's tide chart and found the range of days I suspected she was killed. The tides corroborated my theory. It wasn't much, but it was progress. The problem now was that it looked like she died in Miami and not in the park boundaries. I'd have to think about how to deal with this. For the time being, I decided to keep this to myself.

The wind had picked up, giving me a wet ride back, and in my frustration I didn't heed my training. The boat crashed into the dock, gouging the spot that was still waiting on the final coat of paint. The five-mile ride in these seas aboard the small open boat had rattled my already tired nerves. Zero's barking was annoying and I tried to ignore him as he bear-rushed me at the dock. My evasive maneuvers failed and I found myself squatting down and petting him. The simple effort made me feel a little better and I rose when Becky approached with Jamie glued to her hip.

"Ray's gonna have a piece of you for that one," she said, moving down the seawall to look at the fresh damage.

"I'll give it a go myself this time. He taught me how to repair it."

She gave me a knowing glance that told me it wasn't as easy as it looked. "We'll see. Where's your new lady friend?"

"She's working," I said, thinking it had been too much business and little pleasure between us in the last few days.

"She's a keeper if you ask me." Thunder boomed and she looked toward the west. "They come up fast this time of year."

I realized I had been so caught up in thinking about the case and cursing the building seas that I had neglected what they fore-told. I followed her gaze to the large anvil-shaped cloud that had just formed. Its black bottom was distinct and a wall of gray rain connected it to the water. If I had come in a few minutes later I could easily have been caught in open water. A sudden gust of wind made me stagger sideways and I found myself with Jamie in my arms. Becky leaned over to retie the lines. The wind was pushing the stern of the boat away from the dock. She grabbed the bitter end of the line and took a turn around the cleat, using the added leverage to muscle the boat back to the dock. Once it was close she took a complete turn and then crisscrossed the lines before making the final turn, which bound the line.

"You got to watch it around here," she said, rising and taking Jamie back.

I had just seen something that bothered me. A fat drop of rain fell, a harbinger of what was to come, and we started down the path together, going our separate ways where it split toward our respective houses. Zero paused at the fork, trying to decide which way to go. Becky gave him a firm command and he sped off toward their house. I was a half-dozen steps late getting to my front door and paid the price of getting caught in a Florida downpour. Dripping wet, I entered the house and stripped off my clothes. After changing and grabbing a beer, I sat out on the covered porch watching the storm. Slowly, a picture began forming in my head.

16

THE RAIN CONTINUED UNTIL DUSK, thwarting my plans to see Justine. It wasn't the rain so much as the visibility that worried me. Wet was wet and I could bring a change of clothes, but running a boat without radar through blinding squalls was dangerous. Even with my decision made, I couldn't help but check the weather radar app on my phone in case a window presented itself.

Just before Justine was due in at work, I called her and apologized. We made plans for her next day off, but I hoped to contrive an excuse to see her sooner.

"Aren't you going to ask me about the picture?"

The conversation had turned work related, but at least she was the instigator. I had thought about how to handle this after seeing her persona change at the office. "I didn't want to push."

"I got rid of those dicks last night, so I had a chance to have a look at it."

"No worries. So, fill me in."

"It's a zinc anode. They're used to stop the galvanic corrosion on boats."

I had the choice of either eating my ego and asking her what that was or Googling it myself. She made the decision easy.

"Different metals in a saltwater environment create a chemical reaction called galvanic corrosion. The weaker metal will give up its electrodes and essentially decay. The zinc plates are made to take the brunt of the corrosion. They're attached to the bottom of the boat and need to be replaced every so often, so it would make sense that Bottoms Up would do that as part of their service."

I didn't get into other parts of their service. Pulling the plate I had taken from the case in Brenda's closet, I fingered it. "This doesn't feel like metal. More like plastic."

"They make them out of aluminum and magnesium as well."

I didn't think it was metal at all. "Any chance you can have a look at this one and tell me what it's made of?"

"We might be able to work something out," she said.

We disconnected, leaving me nothing to do but ponder the case. My stomach grumbled and I set the zinc plate down on the table.

I cut up the leftover lobster in small chunks and added some pepper, onions, and a few eggs. The omelet turned out to be a good one. After grabbing a fresh beer, I took a notebook and sat at the counter staring at my laptop wondering where to start. I did Google zinc anodes and got a quick education on the science and what was available. I saw what looked like the six-by-three-inch plate I had and enlarged the image. Pulling the one I had closer, I knew something was wrong. There was no manufacturer's name or model number embossed in the plate like in the pictures—it looked homemade. Without a way to analyze the material, I set it back down and tried a different angle.

First I listed the names across a piece of paper: Abbey, Brenda, Gordy, Herb, Holly, and Gabe. I started drawing lines and circles connecting the players and in a few minutes had a Venn diagram nightmare. It made sense that most of the characters knew each other. My next step was to look at the relationships and try to find a motive.

The only reason I could think of for anyone to kill Abbey was that she had discovered something. Herb and Holly were hurting financially and her rent had to help. The almost-divorced Brenda appeared to be living large, although I knew this meant nothing. Gordy was the sponge of the group but seemed to be the only one smart or sober enough to hatch any kind of plan. If the strange zinc plate was indeed involved, it further implicated him. I tended to side with Gabe. Having been through a divorce, I felt his pain. I knew I would have to put that aside or it would cloud my judgment. Originally, I had discounted Brenda as too weak. But watching Becky use leverage instead of strength to handle the boat had changed my opinion on that.

My head was spinning from all of it. Usually, when this happened, activity was the answer; let your body do something different and your subconscious can take over. Walking to the sliding door, I looked out at the sheets of water pouring off the roof. I wasn't going anywhere.

Another beer and back at the computer, I looked at the list again. I was pretty sure Brenda and Holly were sisters but had never confirmed it. It took a few minutes of searching online to find them. My efforts were rewarded when their maiden names came up the same. I took another look outside and dove into each person's financials, starting with the address of Herb and Holly's house. It was past due on property taxes and would probably be auctioned from underneath them if they didn't sell soon. I found a record of Brenda and Gabe's divorce filing in the courthouse database, but nothing financially. Same for Gordy—if that was his real name.

The motive had to be either love or money—more roughly stated as sex or greed. Beside revenge, there is not much else in the human psyche that triggers the emotional response to take a life.

Herb and Holly were broke and both unemployed and with their drinking habits, unemployable. Brenda was living on her access to Gabe's money. That would stop when the divorce was final. The roulette wheel stopped spinning and money appeared to be the winner. I still had to figure out how Abbey fit into the mix. As it turned out I knew nothing about her personal life. For all I knew she could have been having an affair with Gabe and Brenda killed her for that. Still there was something odd about the zinc plate and my gut told me she was a pawn; a way to accomplish something. Being family only made her death seem colder.

I wasn't quite through patting myself on the back when the phone buzzed. Justine's number came up and I answered, trying to count how many beers I'd had and hoping she wouldn't hear them in my voice.

"Hey, still raining out there?"

"Like crazy. You wouldn't believe it. It'd be pretty cool if you were here."

"Aw shucks, that's sweet."

I paused for a minute, doubting she had called to chat. One of the things I liked about her was her quiet demeanor. She didn't need conversation to fill every hole in her life. "How's work going?"

"Getting caught up. I guess the rain is bad for the crime business too. Gave me some time to look at our stuff and I dug out the wetsuit."

"I thought the evidence would be no good after it dried out."

"Some, yes. But I found some hair samples on it. Neoprene is like a magnet."

I had almost forgotten about the wetsuit. Abbey had been found wearing it; if there was evidence on it, it could be a link to the murderer. "What's it look like?"

"The saltwater has degraded them significantly, and letting it dry out didn't help either. There are some tests that I can do, but without a sample to compare them to, there's not much to be gained. I can't tell unless we run a DNA test whether the strands are male or female, but I compared them to the samples we have on Abbey and I am pretty certain they belong to someone else."

I wished I could be there with her, then wondered if it was creepy to want to share a microscope with the same woman you wanted to share a bed with. "Long or short?" I asked—that was all I had.

"Maybe shoulder length. I don't think that's any help though. Could be a long-haired man or come from anywhere on a woman's head. Sorry, I'm not sounding like this is really helping."

"No, any idea what color?"

"That's a bit unusual. Abbey's hair retained the pigment. The male hair is dark, but the woman's has almost no color. You can almost see through it."

"Hair dye?"

"Probably. That help?"

I looked down at my pad and the women's names. Both Holly and Brenda were at that age where they were likely to dye their hair. "Kind of narrows things down."

"If you want to make a wild-ass guess without any conclusive tests."

I was grasping for straws and I sensed she knew it. Maybe it was the beers, but I hoped I hadn't pushed too far. "See you tomorrow?"

"You bet. Get some sleep. You sound tired."

We said goodbye and disconnected. I noticed it was quiet now. A metal roof lets you know what the weather is like without going outside. Sometime during our conversation, the rain had stopped. I went to the sliding glass door and looked outside. The weather had passed, leaving a crystal-clear sky, something you almost never saw there in the summer. Out west, it was like this most nights, and away from the lights, the Milky Way was often visible.

The sliver of the moon above the horizon highlighted the small waves. The whitecaps were gone and the water looked tranquil.

Slipping on my flip-flops, I left the house to check on the boat. I had learned quickly that though boats and cars had a lot in common, boats needed to be looked after in a way that cars didn't. Walking down to the dock, I checked the lines and made sure the bilge pump and scuppers had done their jobs. Everything looked okay, and I went back inside.

I paced the floor for a few minutes before I came to the conclusion that it was futile to stay. I needed action, and the smallness of the house and island, something I had longed for when I arrived, was making me restless since I knew the murder was not going to get solved while I sat there.

The schedule I had made for Martinez lay on the counter, and I looked at tomorrow's promised area. I had intended to patrol the outer islands as far north as the Ragged Keys. The route led me to a good jumping-off point for a run to Miami. I thought about it for a second, trying to gauge what Martinez's reaction would be if he found out I had patrolled at night. I could easily tell him that a boater had stopped at the dock after the storm with a story of suspicious activity and I had followed up. With the track-course option enabled on the GPS, I could even prove it to him.

Transportation once I got to the mainland would be an issue. A straight shot across the bay to headquarters was the fastest and easiest way. The problem was the keys to the vehicles were locked in the office. Martinez had never given me a key, leaving that a dead end until business hours. If I wanted to do something tonight, a boat ride to Government Cut was the best option. I texted Justine and she agreed to pick me up. We could go back to the lab and look at the zinc and hair together. I smiled, thinking I might just get my microscope date after all.

I texted her my plan and changed clothes. Stuffing the last of the lobster in my mouth and downing a big glass of water to cut through the beer in my system, I left the house and went to the boat.

It was strange being out on the water alone at night. My senses were alive as the hull coasted over the ink-black water. The only light came from the moon and the phosphorescent trail in my wake. Using the GPS chart plotter to navigate, I stayed well away from land and could only tell where the Keys were by the few lights on in the Park Service buildings and bathrooms at the campgrounds.

It was quiet. My report would have no mention of anything of interest. Once I cleared Sands Key, I could see the open Atlantic to starboard. The usual white dots showing the fishing boats on the reef were missing tonight, probably scared off by the storms. I headed toward the mainland, steering a straight line to the markers at the entrance to Government Cut.

Half an hour later, when I had the boat secured to the dock on Dodge Island, Justine pulled up with a smile on her face. I got in and reached for her hand. She pulled it away, leaned in, and kissed me.

The zinc plate in my pocket jabbed into my groin, breaking the moment.

Before I could say anything, she pulled away from the curb and sped toward the 836. The traffic was light and she was driving like Sid on steroids. I just hung on as we flew across the causeway. I left her to drive, not wanting to disrupt her concentration with conversation. Anything I said could have killed us.

Fifteen minutes later, we reached her office, and I exhaled.

I followed her down to the lab and she explained her excitement. "There are some paint chips on the wetsuit that might tie Abbey to the *Big Bang*."

An image appeared on the computer monitor. "Paint?"

"When the wetsuit dried out there were these small chips that came to the surface."

"Are you thinking that rubbed off the bottom of the last boat she cleaned?"

"Bingo. Divers clean their wetsuits after every dive."

"So, if I collect samples from the bottom of the *Big Bang*, we might get a direct connection and establish the boat as a crime scene?"

"Well, that's where the detective work comes in." She said it like a coach putting you in the game with every confidence you would have a positive impact.

"This might help too." I pulled the zinc out of my pocket and set it on the table.

"Right on," she said, picking it up and twirling it in her hands. She set it down and handed me an evidence bag and a pair of blue nitrile gloves. "You go check on the boat paint, and I'll run this and see what we have."

"Borrow your car?"

She smiled and handed me the keys. "No worries, I can get a patrol to take me home if you're not back."

I felt a tinge of jealousy at the thought of a uniformed officer putting her to bed.

17

BACKWATER
BAY

WITH A FEW HOURS before dawn I decided to pay Sid a visit and see if he would revisit the cause of death. The only problem was he wasn't there.

In his place was a hip-looking young man, I guess what you would call a hipster. His hair and mustache both were too well groomed for my taste and clearly required a whole lot of product to hold their form. I guessed he'd have been wearing a plaid shirt and too-tight jeans if he weren't in scrubs. I felt my thirty-eight years when I judged him too young to be a doctor. That quick decision almost cost me. "Is Sid around?" Fortunately, I used his name instead of asking for the generic medical examiner.

"Vance Able." He held out his hand. "Chief medical examiner. What can I do for you?" he asked, eyeing my uniform.

"Kurt Hunter with the National Park Service. I'm the special agent for Biscayne."

"Biscayne—cool, man. Sid's off tonight. I'm filling in."

His voice had just a twinge of squeakiness to it that was slightly irritating. Not enough to sound like nails on a blackboard, but enough to be noticeable. It didn't do anything to establish his credibility, in fact quite the opposite. The voice in my head told me not to judge. "I had a body come in that was labeled a Jane Doe. I think Justine from the crime lab confirmed the identity as Abbey Bentley. During the autopsy, Sid ruled it an accidental death. I wanted to talk to your office about some evidence we've collected that it might be a homicide."

"Sid is the man. Guess it gets lonely down here at night. I bet he let you help. Hey, you get to fish much?"

He led me over to a computer monitor and asked for the name again. It came up as Abbey Bentley and not Jane Doe. I had to convince him now or I would lose the body.

He studied the screen for a few minutes, clicking on several images that showed the propeller wounds. "Gnarly. And you think this happened postmortem? Bruising would signify the sequence. Sid knows his stuff."

"She was in the water for almost ten days before the body was found."

"That makes it harder."

"I have a theory that she was murdered."

"Go ahead...."

He was all business now. I took a breath, knowing I probably only had one shot at this. "He noted during the autopsy that there were visible signs of overexpansion to her lungs. She was using scuba gear to clean a boat bottom at the time of death. I think the murderer held her in place with the air line while depressing the purge button on the regulator."

"Interesting. I'm more of a fisherman than a diver. Your knowledge of scuba equipment is good enough to support this?"

"I had an expert run through it with me." I had his interest now.

"I'll make a deal," he said, looking at the file.

I nodded.

"Got any hot bonefish spots?"

I paused for a second, knowing where this was going. "A few. I've only been here a month so I'm just learning the water."

"Awesome, dude. I've been trying to figure out the fly scene lately."

I wondered when fly fishing had gotten hip. "I'm just learning the saltwater thing. Most of my experience is the streams out west."

"You think you could take me out someday?"

"Sure," I said, trying to figure out how to steer the conversation back to Abbey. "We can give it a shot." I guessed Martinez would be okay with my sucking up to the chief medical examiner, but I figured I better not get his expectations too high. "Bonefish is a hit-or-miss business though." He took the bait and looked back at the screen. I watched over his shoulder while he worked. Once he focused on his work, he appeared older.

I inched closer to see the screen. He was scrolling through the report faster than I could keep up.

"Sid followed procedure. The lungs were clearly damaged by overexpansion, but the major trauma was the propeller wound. With the body in such a decomposed state, he went with the overwhelming evidence. There was no sign of a struggle—not that there wasn't one, but if there was, it just wasn't visible because of the state of her body."

"She was wearing a wetsuit. There are some hair strands belonging to someone else as well as paint smudges." I summarized Justine's findings.

"I'm not going to change Sid's finding." He paused. "I will talk to him though."

That was the best I could hope for.

"So, the bonefishing gig?" he asked as I walked out the door.

"Yeah, sure," I said abruptly, maybe harsher than I should have. I guessed that he was only a few years younger than me, but it felt like a generation. The hipster deal had never appealed to me.

Back on the street, it was still dark. The screen of my phone was blank—no texts or messages from Justine. I decided against bothering her about work now. She would likely be asleep. I was tired as well but with the body now having an identity, I was out of time.

With no destination in mind, I found myself driving toward Coral Gables. Herb and Holly's house was dark, although a few of the neighbors already had lights on. Driving past their block, I found a coffee shop just opening and bought a large cup, water, and a few energy bars. I used the restroom and drove back to the house. It was just starting to get light when I returned. This early in the morning there was little going on. A few early joggers and the lights in several kitchen windows were the only signs of life. With a cup of gas station coffee between my legs, I sat in the truck and watched the street wake up. It was a slow process. School must not have started yet because that wave of activity never came.

There was no action at the house until after the stroller brigade had done their meet-and-greet and taken a few laps around the block. It was then that I saw the first sign of activity. Holly made the first appearance, dressed like almost every woman I had seen. Her outfit said yoga all over it. From what I had seen of the stroller brigade earlier, that was no indication that yoga was in the forecast. She got in her Jeep Grand Cherokee and pulled out of the driveway. I let her go. It was Herb that I was interested in.

An hour later, Herb wandered out with a cup of coffee and climbed into his basic blue Honda Civic. I followed at a distance. With no idea where he was heading, I kept close enough to catch any quick turns and far enough back that my vehicle, thankfully a plain white, didn't catch his eye. My inexperience at tailing didn't matter as he seemed oblivious. He turned onto South Dixie Highway, the local name for US 1, and after a few blocks turned into a strip center. Parking in front of a plain storefront with a sign that said DELANY AND COMPANY—INSURANCE, he exited the car and went inside.

The large windows kept me from going over to scope the place out. Instead, I checked the website for Delany and Company. Their specialties included every kind of insurance you could think of. I scrolled down the list. From the tax lien on their home and the age of the cars they drove there was no reason to need an agent for their insurance. Unless you were totally inept, that was all easily done over the Internet. RV and boat insurance were non-starters, and then I saw life insurance—something you couldn't buy online.

My phone rang and the screen changed, showing a local number. I hit *Accept* and heard Sid's voice. "So, I see you met Vance."

Sid's strong Jersey accent was loud and clear. So was his mood. "I didn't mean to step on your toes. We just started talking."

"Well, he's all excited about you taking him fishing. I never understood this fly-fishing, 'catch-and-release' thing he keeps talking about. I'm more of a bluefish and striper kind of guy. Seems like you're his new best friend."

I had a vision of Sid standing on a rocky shore with a surf rod, stooped over and casting into a biting wind. "Believe me, that was nothing I was trying to come away with."

I relaxed the death grip on my phone when he laughed.

"Yeah, the boy can be a little eager." He cleared his throat and changed the subject. "He explained your theory about the woman's death being a homicide."

"Is there any way to really tell the order of what happened?"

"Not after the body had been in the water for so long. If it was fresh, it would be easy. The bruising and clotting around the stomach wounds would have indicated whether the propeller strike was pre - or postmortem. With all the blood washed away and the damage to the wound by the water and crabs, it's virtually impossible."

I let that hang in the air, thinking it better to allow him to reach his own conclusion.

"As long as I have room in the cooler, I'll play along. See what you can come up with."

"Thanks. I owe you for this," I said. It was as good of an outcome as I could have expected.

"They say payback is a bitch. In this case it's going to be Vance. I'll let you know when I need him out of my hair and you can take the boy fishing."

I thanked him despite the promise. When I looked up, Herb's car was still parked where he had left it. I glanced at my watch and saw it was almost nine o'clock. There was no way to see what was going on in the office and I had a schedule to keep.

Everything changed when my phone rang again. This time it was Martinez demanding an audience. I pulled out and headed south on South Dixie. It was the slower but more direct route, and I arrived at the Park Service headquarters at 9:40. Just in time to see Susan McLeash pull in ahead of me.

I cursed my bad luck, but there was nothing I could do now. She was waiting by the truck door when I opened it. When we were side by side, she stood almost as tall as me and damned near as wide.

"I guess you know the boss is looking for you."

I saw the smile on her face and went inside. When I waved at Mariposa, she looked down instead of giving me her standard greeting. With Susan on my heels, I headed upstairs.

"Freelancing is not acceptable," he started.

I sensed Susan behind me and could guess there was a smile on her face.

"All these people you're bothering have bosses and unlike you, they file reports and submit time sheets. It seems the Park Service, and by that I mean you, has been making the rounds."

"I have enough evidence to make this a homicide." It was the only thing I could say in my own defense.

"That old-man coroner went along with you and changed the cause of death?" he asked.

"Not officially, but he gave me a few days."

The ball was rolling now. He decided to get out of its way. "Any leads then?" he asked.

In an instant he had changed his attitude. Even if Abbey's death remained accidental, the Park Service had done well in establishing her identity. It might catch a small blurb in the back section of the newspaper. Should the death become a homicide it would land on the front page. I knew Martinez loved the spotlight and he sensed it now. The only problem was we had to clear the case.

"We have a crime scene and I'm working on several suspects."

"Motive?" he asked.

"Her aunt and uncle, whom she was living with, are having money trouble. In fact the man was at an insurance agency this morning. Then there's the divorce of her aunt and a million-dollar boat."

Not knowing if Martinez was trying to push me out of the investigation, I was hesitant and purposefully kept some names and details out. Susan had sat in the seat beside me and was taking notes. When I finished, he looked at both of us. I thought I was done.

"Susan will be working with you the rest of the way," he said.

I didn't have to look over to know there was a grin on her face.

18

STEVEN BECKER

A KURT HUNTER MYSTERY

BACKWATER
BAY

UNFORTUNATELY, it didn't end there. As if to justify inserting Susan into the case, he spent fifteen minutes recounting everything I had done against regulations since starting there. When he was done, I doubted if I would have let myself work without supervision. After being fully dressed down, Martinez reinforced his order that I work with Susan and dismissed us.

We faced off in the hallway. I looked over at her and saw the smile lines entrenched in her makeup and had to stifle a laugh. There was no way I was going to let her get involved with the people or evidence. My only play was to have her fill an actual need, and do something she was good at. I asked her to follow up on the insurance angle and gave her the agent's name and address. This got me out of the building and I almost ran to the boat.

Figuring a shower and change of clothes were not negotiable, I took the boat from the slip and headed out the channel into open water. Susan McLeash. The name played over and over in my mind. Even the windblown air coming off the still water of the bay couldn't wash it from my conscience. I had been played and I knew it.

I wouldn't have put it past Susan to have been watching the GPS in the Park Service truck and the boat. She probably knew every move I had made and would freely use them against me. Call me paranoid, but since I'd been there I'd already had a run-in with a bad cop. Martinez was a known quantity though, riding out his time in his air-conditioned office until he could collect his pension. He knew the game and how to play it, and Susan McLeash was his tool. Her agenda was different.

The dock at Adams Key came into sight and an image of Martinez sitting in his padded chair watching me on his monitor came to me at the same time. I cut the wheel to starboard.

It was as clear as the six-foot-deep water that Martinez and McLeash were conspiring to take credit should the investigation reach a successful conclusion. The opposite was also clear: if it failed I would be the one to take the fall. With that in mind, I played back the conversation in Martinez's office, trying to remember what Susan had written so precisely in her notebook.

I had left the paper trail to her. I had to throw her a bone and I figured it was better to toss the one that I had no idea what to do with. After fixing her makeup to remove the smile lines, she was probably sitting at her ultra-neat desk in front of her disinfected computer station scanning whatever documents she could get her hands on. I'd given up the names of the players but had left the relationships vague. I wasn't above accepting help. Maybe she could come up with the motive I was missing.

In the meantime, I would do the unexpected—my job. Justine was likely asleep until at least noon. Even if I were to scrape the boat bottom and bring her the evidence, she wouldn't be able to analyze it until she went into work at five. With no message from her last night, I had to assume she hadn't had time to analyze the zinc plate either.

My schedule had me south today and I cruised past Totten Key at twenty knots. There was a narrow cut to the Atlantic at Old

Rhodes Key that I decided to check out. It was one of those deep channels to nowhere between Old Rhodes and Swan Key that suddenly and without an explanation ended in two feet of water just a hundred yards from deep water. The real pass was a quarter mile south between Swan and Broad Keys. After checking the old channel, I idled over to the marked cut. It wasn't one of the main passes in the park. Narrow, with shallow flats adjacent to it on both sides, it was dangerous if you didn't know the water. I'd already helped more than one boater off the sandbars there.

It was quiet today, and I had stopped in mid channel by Broad Creek when I saw a half dozen fins slice through the still water. My heart leapt and I almost reached for the rod I had stashed inside the console. Coming to my senses, I filed the spot away for another day, noting the stage of the tide that had brought the fish in. This would be where I would take Vance when that debt came due. Resuming my patrol, I idled through to the Atlantic side and stopped. Surprised to see only a few boats fishing or lobstering the patch reefs, I had just turned to the north to complete my loop when I saw the shrimper.

She was heading in, just to the south of my position. A commercial fishing boat moving in this direction into the south bay was unusual and set off alarms. Using the mangrove shoreline for cover, I watched the boat approach. It appeared headed for a narrow pass frequented by some of the flats guides. The area was a maze of narrow creeks running between the Atlantic and bay. I'd heard about this being a smugglers' haven and proceeded carefully.

Removing my gun belt from the console, I put it around my waist with one hand while I steered with the other. When I checked the gauges, everything looked normal. I spun the wheel and headed back to the bay. I was out of sight of the shrimper and used the speed and shallow draft of the center-console to my advantage. I made it to the bay side first and turned toward

Angelfish Creek, where the shrimper had disappeared. I wasn't surprised after fifteen minutes that it hadn't emerged yet. Even if I had radar, the landmass the boat was hidden in would still conceal it. It was a perfect hideout. There was nothing I could do except pursue.

Before I did this, I pulled my phone out of the cargo pocket on my shorts and was about to press Martinez's number to call in my position, and request backup, when I saw I had no service. I'd been down this far several times and knew I was in the No Man's Land between the towers of North Key Largo and Homestead.

Picking up the microphone clipped to the dashboard, I turned up the volume on the VHF and called in on channel 16. Mariposa answered and seconds later, after switching to channel 17, I had Martinez on the line.

If there was another lecture coming, I didn't get it. He knew enough to hold his tongue on the open channel and we talked in obtuse terms. Any smuggler would have his VHF on scan mode and could easily hear our conversation. With the aid of his tracker, we didn't have to disclose my location and in a few minutes backup was on the way.

This was ICE—Immigration and Customs Enforcement— territory. My role was to monitor the situation until they could get there. Fortunately, with their assets, I didn't have to wait long. Within a half hour, I heard the thump-thump of a helicopter and the engines of one of their go-fast boats. Several minutes after I heard it, the boat pulled next to me. The fenders of the Interceptor 39 barely reached the gunwales of my boat and we bobbed together uneasily for a few minutes until the captain called down for me to anchor my boat and board.

I dropped the Power-Pole and crossed to the larger boat. It was almost twice the size of mine and was loaded with weapons and electronics. The only thing missing was a mounted fifty-caliber gun. I felt naked after seeing the four men aboard, dressed in their bulletproof vests with assault rifles clipped to a sling.

"Johnny Wells," the captain said, extending his hand.

I took it and introduced myself to him and his men. "How do you want to handle this?" They gathered around and I quickly laid out the situation.

The helicopter had pulled off so as not to alert the shrimper. The captain called them back for a quick pass. A few minutes later, the chopper confirmed the shrimper was sitting in one of the creeks and they had seen bales on the deck.

"We're gonna need to work together on this," Johnny said.

I glanced at my watch, already paranoid about being out of cell range with Susan McLeash on the loose. "What can I do?"

"This hog draws too much water for the creeks. We need you and your boat to get in there."

I wasn't sure how Martinez was going to take this. Repairing bullet holes in the Park Service boat was not going to complement his budget. I looked at the radio. It was the only way to reach him and I couldn't think of any way to discreetly convey what the ICE agents were asking. All eyes were on me as I vacillated. I knew helping was the right thing to do, even if it was my ego that made the decision.

"Right on. Let's go get 'em," I said. Several minutes later one of the men Johnny had assigned to stay aboard the Interceptor maneuvered the larger boat next to mine, and Johnny and another agent climbed across the gunwales with me. They must have seen me looking enviously at their bulletproof vests. Johnny asked one of the men to toss one over. I caught it and slid it over my head.

The larger boat pulled away.

"There are at least six creeks in there," Johnny said, pointing to the maze of mangroves in front of us. "It looks like they all run to both the bay and ocean sides. I'm going to station the Interceptor on the outside and we'll cover the shallower water on the inside with your boat. Then I'll call back the chopper to chase them out."

It made sense. The only problem I could see with his plan was what the smugglers were doing in there in the first place. Chances were, if they had continued along the barrier islands and turned inland near Key Biscayne, they'd be home by now. "Why are they holed up in there?" I asked.

"They usually wait until dark. Then several of these bad boys"—he nodded at the go-fast boat—"will run out and off-load the shrimper. Split the load and split the risk."

I had to assume these men knew their business. A quick look at the sky confirmed it was only noonish. There was plenty of time before we would have company. Johnny knew we'd have the advantage if we acted now. With both boats in place, he called in the chopper.

A few minutes later the helicopter was in sight. The water vibrated as it descended and made a sweep of the cluster of islands. They were low enough that I could see the focused look on the man behind the machine gun in the open door. They passed us and dropped another few feet. Suddenly they seemed to hang in the air and I heard a voice over a loudspeaker. The chopper was too far away to make out what was being said, but I had a good idea.

Johnny tapped me on the shoulder and nodded forward. It was time to move. At idle speed, I crept into Angelfish Creek and entered the smaller creek at Linderman Key. I saw the tower of the shrimper and was starting to head toward it when I felt a hand on my shoulder.

"He'll make a move. Best not to get cornered in there," Johnny said.

I stopped and let the current take us into the mangroves. The ICE agents held us in place by grabbing branches and together we waited. It was quiet now that the helicopter had moved off and hovered about a quarter mile from us waiting for orders. The shrimper must have sensed their chance and decided to make a run for it. The engine started, emitting a cloud of black smoke, and the center-console swayed in the wake pushed ahead of the larger boat as they came toward us.

The bow came in sight and the ICE agents raised their weapons. Feeling secure in the bulletproof vest, I remained at the wheel waiting for the boat to make its move. Johnny reached for the microphone. I saw his intent and switched from VHF to the hailer. He called out for the boat to stop and the crew to assemble on the bow with their hands up.

There was some confusion on the shrimper and time started to slip by. I thought if they were going to surrender they would have already. Looking over at Johnny, I got the sense that he felt this too. He picked up the microphone again and called in the helicopter.

The chopper came toward us. A stream of bullets pierced the water alongside the hull of the shrimper. Looking up at the chopper circling overhead I saw a smile cross the face of the man behind the gun. There was movement on the shrimper again. A group of eight men huddled in the bow with their hands up. I felt the thrill of victory, but looking at the agents on board, I thought that might have been premature.

Johnny, still with the microphone in his hand, brought it up and gave direction to the crew. A few minutes later, they were following us out of the creek and through the pass into deeper water. The Interceptor circled several times and the shrimper dropped anchor.

The agents handled the transfer efficiently, and quickly had the crew of the shrimper aboard the Interceptor and two of their men on the shrimper. Johnny thanked me and handed me his card. An hour after it had started, I was left alone.

I was feeling good, like I had actually accomplished something, when the markers for Caesar Creek came into sight.

Turning to starboard and deeper water, I cruised far enough to catch the green #1 marker and cut the wheel hard to port. Following the channel in, I was starting to think about my next move when my phone dinged. And dinged again. And another half-dozen times until I realized I had been out of reception for the last few hours. Whatever I had gained in helping ICE bust the shrimper was lost being out of the loop on my own investigation.

I glanced at the messages and looked at my watch; it was almost two. Several were from Justine, letting me know that she was up and wanted to talk. There was nothing from Susan McLeash.

19

STEVEN BECKER

A KURT HUNTER MYSTERY

BACKWATER BAY

I TEXTED Martinez a picture of the ICE agents aboard the shrimper with the Park Service boat in the foreground. Johnny had taken it from the Interceptor and sent it to me as a thank-you. The phone rang seconds later. It didn't take a rocket scientist to figure out that good publicity greased the grooves for politically minded bureaucrats. Martinez took the bait like a snapper after a shrimp.

"That's some actual work you did there this morning. I just got the report from the ICE agent in charge that you were very help-ful," he said.

"Just in the right place at the right time," I said, knowing it was pretty much the truth. I had done nothing but make a call.

"Anyway. There was a couple hundred thousand worth of weed and coke on the shrimper—big enough to make the news."

That was why he was so happy. I didn't figure I would play prominently, or even at all, in the reports, but that was okay. Anonymity was my friend, especially after my run-in with the cartel that ran the pot grow. "Glad it worked out." I paused, ready to press my advantage. "I haven't heard from Susan yet." The line was silent for a minute. I heard the squeak of his chair and guessed he had turned to face his dual monitors.

"Give me a few minutes and I'll see what I can find out."

I thanked him and looked out at the water. Still without the shower and change of clothes I had promised myself, I coasted up to the concrete dock at Adams Key and tied off the boat. Zero was tuned in as usual and came bounding toward me with Becky following.

"Must be gettin' the hang of it. Only the damned dog heard you."

I could hear the baby crying.

"Woke Jamie up though."

I knew what she wanted. "I'll take Zero for a while. Probably only be here for an hour or so though."

"That hour of peace'll get you a free lunch. Just about to fry up some snapper that Ray brought in yesterday."

Growing up in California, it was bred into me to avoid anything with bread crumbs and grease. Becky had shown me early on the error of my ways. With her light touch, the fish was excellent. "You're on. I'll take Zero and come by in a while."

"Thanks, Kurt," she said, making a beeline for the house. The screen door slammed and a minute later the crying stopped.

I looked down at Zero. "Come on, boy." On the walk up the path to my house I tried to explain to him how babies are tough on dogs, but once Jamie was a few years older, he'd have a friend. Our family dog had gone through the same thing after Allie was born. "It'll get better in a year or so." I'm not sure how he took it, but it made me sad thinking about Allie as a baby and how much I missed her now.

Once inside, I tossed my clothes in the washer and headed for the shower. Standing under the spray of the hot water, I thought about what I needed to do next. Having Susan McLeash "helping" was troubling and I figured she should be my first call. I shut the water off, got out, and started to dry myself off. There was a faint smell of Justine on the towel, and my attention got sidetracked.

Shaved and dressed, I went to the breakfast bar in the kitchen and checked my email. Several messages loaded and I scanned them for anything from Susan. It was a good thing I had no expectations, as there was nothing from my new "helper." I was also surprised there was nothing from Martinez. He was one of those desk jockeys who documented everything and email was a perfect mechanism for this. With all the CCs and BCCs, it was easy to make it look like you were on top of things.

Zero was snoring on the floor and I walked by without waking him. Becky would know where to find him. Leaving the house unlocked, I went to the dock, thinking there was nothing to be accomplished sitting out there on the island. There was no sign of life from her house as I pulled the boat away and eased the bow into the channel.

Just as I was about to start across the bay, my phone vibrated in my pocket. Martinez's name flashed across the screen. Dropping to neutral, I watched the drift of the boat for a second before cutting the engine and answering.

"Susan's vehicle has been idle for almost two hours. Her phone is turned off."

It sounded like she was in trouble. "Where?"

"The marina off Alton."

"I thought she was just going to do some computer work and research," I said, wondering if she had gone out on her own or if Martinez had authorized her to take over the case.

"She can be a little hard to control sometimes," he said.

My success earlier today must have restored his confidence in me. I knew Susan covered his back when he left early to play golf or came in late after a night out. Maybe there was more to it. He sounded like he was actually worried. "I'm on my way in," I said, and disconnected.

Starting the engine, I pushed the throttle to the stop. The boat seemed as eager as I was. The bow jumped out of the water, followed quickly by the stern. Seconds later, I was running at close to thirty knots. It was the hardest I had pushed the boat and the fastest I had gone. It was exhilarating, and I couldn't help but feel empowered. For the first time since I had started there, I felt I had the upper hand on Martinez. All I could hope was that Susan was not in trouble or screwing with my case.

Martinez was in the lobby looking like he was heading to a photo op with his dress uniform on. Along with his counterpart at ICE, he'd be on the news tonight standing behind a table stacked high with drugs and weapons. It bothered me a little that neither Johnny or I would be there. His presence precluded the usual small talk with Mariposa. She handed me the keys to the Park Service truck and I was out the door.

I had slipped into the doldrums between lunch and rush-hour traffic. The ride to Miami was slow but uneventful. I pulled into the parking lot for the marina and checked my phone. It was after four already, and I realized I had not called Justine yet. Texting her to see if she had a minute, I cruised the parking lot until I found the Park Service car.

The doors were locked and nothing seemed out of place. Back at the truck, I texted Martinez to let him know I had located the car and saw a missed call from Justine. Susan could have been in danger, so I decided to return the call while I walked to the docks.

Justine listened intently as I recounted the morning's adventure. The takedown of the shrimper was a nonstarter for her. It was a little disappointing when she almost yawned over the phone. I knew it was forensics that rocked her boat and was about to ask if she'd had any luck with the evidence when I stepped onto the edge of the dock, looked over to where the *Big Bang* had been berthed, and breathed a sigh of relief that the boat was still there.

"I gotta go," I said, starting toward the boat. "I'll get that paint sample for you."

"Cool. Did you get my message about the zinc plate you brought in?"

I had been wondering why she hadn't said anything. "I didn't. Must have gotten lost when I was out of service this morning." I looked down at my phone and scrolled through the messages. There was a text from her this morning that I must have missed when they all came in together. "I just saw it. That thing is made of C-4?"

"Yes, sir, had to call the bomb squad in and everything. They said it was inert until there was a detonator attached in case you're wondering."

"Really? Are you okay?"

"It was a bit of a scare, but what are those guys up to?"

That was a good question, and the insurance angle was starting to make sense. I thought for a second. "Susan was supposed to be looking into an insurance thing." I explained to her how I had followed Herb that morning. I thanked her and promised to bring the paint sample by as soon as possible. Now I had to find Susan.

There was no activity on deck, and with my hand on my sidearm, I approached the ship. Standing alongside, I could hear voices, one of which I was sure was Susan's. Moving forward, I slammed my foot into the bollard that housed the electrical, phone, and cable hookups. My boat shoes absorbed the brunt of it, but looking at the two thick yellow cords coming from the bottom of the box and running over the rail of the ship, I got an idea.

Going into the salon, even with my sidearm, was risky. I had no idea how many people were in there, what their mood was, or if they were armed. It was much safer to have them come out on deck. The first cable stuck when I pulled. Leaning over to see what the problem was, I noticed the twist-lock receptacle. Immediately I could hear the air-conditioner cut off when the plug was pulled. I twisted and removed the other line which I guessed handled the rest of the shore power.

The boat shifted slightly. There was still no one visible, but something was going on. Still not sure who was aboard, I stepped backward, trying to find some cover. The salon door opened, and I shrank back.

Susan McLeash emerged by herself onto the back deck. She took a quick look around and stepped up to the dock. I turned my back to the pedestal and the boat, hoping she was focused on leaving and would not see me. Slowly I risked a look behind me and froze when I heard my phone ring in my pocket. I reached into my pocket and disconnected the call hoping no one had heard it. I slid the toggle to vibrate. The phone went quiet and I looked back to the dock. Susan hadn't noticed anything. She had already turned the corner and was heading to the marina.

She was the only one who had exited and I still wanted to know who was aboard. Though I was concerned with what Susan was up to, she was one of the good guys. I had a feeling she had heard about my exploits with ICE this morning and was after her own fifteen minutes of fame. Little did she know that Martinez would take it from her.

I decided to watch the boat instead of following her. As long as Martinez was on my side, at least for now, I thought I could at least use him to track her, but looking at my watch, and seeing it was almost five o'clock, I had my doubts he would even be around. There was usually a mandatory stop at a bar at the end of a news conference. Deciding I had nothing to lose, I dialed his number and wasn't disappointed when it went to voicemail.

From the corner of my eye, I saw the white Park Service car pull out of the parking lot. It was too late to see what Susan was up to, so I picked a spot in the shade with a clear view of the *Big Bang* and called Justine.

"Sorry about that," I started to explain.

"No worries. I figured it was work. Want dinner?"

I realized I had forgotten to stop by Becky's and had never had lunch. "Yup. Let me grab that paint sample and I'll be over." I went back to the truck and grabbed the evidence bag from the seat, then started back to the *Big Bang*.

"Ahoy there," I called out, feeling like an idiot again. There had to be a better way to hail a boat. A long minute went by and I hailed again. Still no answer. If there was someone aboard, they were playing possum. If there wasn't, Susan had been doing an illegal search. That might explain why her car had been there so long and her phone wasn't turned on. I filed that away to confront her with later. I took a look around, then got to my knees to collect the sample. Unable to reach below the waterline, I had to lie on my stomach to scrape the paint into the bag. When I got up the dockmaster was staring at me.

"You folks are awfully busy around here today."

I didn't know if he really had something on me or if he was just doing his job and watching the boats. "Just getting a paint sample."

"I guess you don't need a warrant for that, but the woman agent was on here by herself."

I knew what he was implying and wondered how much trouble Susan had gotten me into now. I brushed myself off and tried to reassure him that everything was just part of a routine investigation. He nodded, and I walked faster than I probably should have to the truck.

STEVEN BECKER

A KURT HUNTER MYSTERY

BACKWATER BAY

I HAD HEARD about how momentum affected a case—when things started rolling on their own, motive, opportunity, and means seemed to work themselves out. I hadn't uncovered any of the three pillars of this crime yet, but I could sense something was about to break.

Stopping at the potted palm by the bar, I looked over surprised to see either Gordy or Brenda. I still hadn't heard from Susan and tried her number again. The call went straight to voicemail. I was starting to worry. Not about her; she could take care of herself. It was more about what she was doing with the case. There were enough wild cards already.

I thought about Martinez, then realized that involving him could complicate things. I already knew the line in his head separating what was good for the service and what was good for him personally was blurry.

I had been standing there staring at the *Big Bang* and thinking about Susan and the case long enough for the shade I had been hiding in to have moved. The sun was already below the buildings across the intracoastal, making me realize I was getting little done sitting there thinking. Glancing over my shoulder at the *Big Bang* sitting in her slip, I turned toward the parking lot. I was walking slowly, procrastinating instead of deciding what my next step should be.

I texted Justine that I was on my way with the paint sample and headed for the truck. It didn't take long until I was at a dead stop. I stared at the traffic. A stream of brake lights was in front of me as far as I could see. It had been a half hour already and I had just made it over the causeway. Finally, I started to pick up speed after passing the exit off the 836 for Marlins Park and guessed there was a game tonight. I expected the natives would have known this and wondered how long it would take me to adjust to big-city life. Justine called, wondering where I was, and redirected me to an Italian place near her office with the explanation that she would be getting "hangry" sooner than I could get there.

I found the restaurant, parked, and walked inside. It appeared to be a family-owned place rather than a chain, which made me happy. I saw her, already seated at a table, and wove my way through the sea of red-and-white-checked tablecloths half-full with diners. Chianti bottles holding lit candles provided most of the lighting. By the time I sat down I was starving.

"I already ordered," Justine said, munching on a breadstick.

We'd just hit level three on the relationship scale. "Cool."

"You look wiped," she said. "Have a beer, you're staying at my place tonight."

I smiled. Definitely level three. We chatted about everything except work, and when the food started arriving, she told me about her paddle that morning as an apology for ordering so much. I was through my second beer and third course when we finally got around to work.

"I can't believe I almost blew you up," I said.

"That was touch and go for a while. I was wondering if that's how you got rid of your girlfriends." She laughed, breaking the tension. "Someone wanted to blow up that boat," she said.

"And I think Abbey was killed when she figured out that the zincs she was replacing were explosives."

"There's your motive. Who would have benefited most from the boat being blown up?" she asked.

I took a sip of my third beer, thankful that I was staying with her tonight. "There's the insurance angle with Herb and Holly." I told her about Herb's visit to the insurance agency that morning. "And Brenda's upcoming divorce." I paused. "Gordy fits in here somewhere too. He's too sleazy to be clean."

"That narrows the field," she said, finishing off her pasta. "What about Gabe, the owner?"

"Yeah, but that's his baby." Suddenly I felt exhausted. I didn't know if I was being overwhelmed by the case, my adventure with ICE, not sleeping for the last few days, or the third beer. Probably a combination of all the above, I thought, and yawned again.

"Come on. I'm taking you home."

I had just enough energy left to pay the check and drive the Park Service truck to the crime lab. I figured that was better than leaving it at the restaurant. Justine drove me to her place.

"Take the bed," she ordered after unlocking the door. "I'll be back in a few hours."

I was past the point of being a gentleman and demanding the couch. In minutes I was asleep.

———

MY PHONE WOKE ME AND IT TOOK A MINUTE FOR ME TO FIGURE OUT where I was. Justine was beside me, under the covers. I lay on top of the comforter just as I had fallen asleep. I leaned on an elbow and looked at the screen, wincing when I saw Martinez's name. Fighting off the magnetic pull of the *Decline* button on my finger, I hit *Accept*, slid out of bed, walked to the living room, and put the phone to my ear.

"It's almost noon. What are you doing in Miami? According to the schedule I have here, submitted by you by the way, the Card Sound Bridge should be closer than Government Cut." Of course, he knew where I was.

I had dug my own hole by sleeping in. A picture flashed through my mind of him at his desk watching the dual computer screens all morning cursing at the icon of the truck sitting in the parking lot. I was actually surprised he had waited this long to call. In that second, I knew how to figure out what Susan was up to, but first I needed to placate Martinez. "I'll head down now."

"I'll be expecting a written report when you're done, for this and every other patrol for the next month."

The subconscious is a powerful tool. In my anger, it took over and I listened to the words coming out of my mouth as if somebody else was speaking them. "I could add the GPS log from the boat to the report, but I don't know how to access the data."

"Now, that's the first good idea you've had this week. I'll email you the instructions."

Before I could answer, the call disconnected. I cursed about the extra paperwork, vowing to keep the reports as boring as possible. Including the logs would limit my ability to fish and free-lance. That was certainly a downside. The upside was once I had the instructions I could see what Susan had been up to. I would bet both her car and boat were also tagged.

Not wanting to wake Justine, I slid out the door and called a cab from the street. While I waited, I remembered Holly's saying something about Herb taking Ubers everywhere. I had never had the need and wasn't familiar with the service. The cab had still not arrived and I pressed the icon for the app store and downloaded the Uber app. In seconds, I was registered, and with no cab in sight, I hit the *Get a Ride* button. The screen changed and said the driver, Irene, would be arriving in three minutes and driving an Acura. The fare listed was less than ten dollars—way cheaper than a cab. Irene arrived before the cab and I settled in for the ride to the crime lab wondering whether the Uber app could be used to trace Herb's movements.

When Irene dropped me off, I thanked her, left a tip on the app, and walked to the truck. Forty minutes later I parked behind the headquarters building and looked around the lot for the car I had seen Susan driving. It sat next to another truck identical to the one I was driving. I thought about touching the hood to see if I could tell from the temperature how long the car had been sitting, but walking toward it I saw the heat shimmering off it. In the South Florida sun, the exercise was pointless.

As much as I wanted a face-off with her, I was not inclined to do it here and let Martinez referee. I already knew what the outcome of that match would be. My moment in the sun with him had ended when the press conference was over. Bypassing the main entrance and the windows of Martinez's and Susan's offices, I walked around the back of the building and stepped onto the dock. Susan's boat sat next to mine, carefully tied. It was almost one o'clock and a beautiful day with a light breeze from the southeast. There was no need for the spiderweb of lines tying off her boat. My guess was that she took these precautions so as not to have to check the boat too often.

With both dock lines loose, I stepped down to my center-console, glanced over at the building to see if I had been seen, and started the engine. Quickly, I hauled the lines aboard and backed out of the slip. When the boat was almost clear of the dock, I eased the throttle forward until it clicked into the neutral position, allowing the boat's momentum to bring it back the remaining half a dozen feet. Once the bow was clear, I idled away from the Park Service docks. The shared inlet with Bayfront Park's ramp kept me focused until I cleared the line of incoming boats and headed toward the bay.

With the last marker behind me, I plotted a course to my assigned patrol area and pushed down the throttle. Skimming over the flat seas, I glanced down at the base of the steering wheel. Martinez's email had arrived with directions to access the GPS logs and as he said, there was a bar code attached to the helm. It was the same size and type that was used on retail packaging.

Knowing the same label was affixed to Susan's boat, I steered toward North Key Largo, pulling back on the throttle as I approached the markers for the skinny channel through Card Bank. Once through the shallow area, I moved toward the coast and set the speed at eleven hundred RPMs. I was eager to get back to the dock and pull the ID numbers from Susan's boat. I pushed the RPMs up to fourteen hundred, the limit of what I thought Martinez would allow for a "thorough patrol," and the boat picked up speed, cruising effortlessly through the calm waters.

The slice of a fin breaking through the surface of the water caught my eye. Under normal circumstances, the Power-Pole would already have been deployed and I would be assembling my rod. Today was the exception, and I set the location in my memory and continued patrolling the mangrove-lined shore. Little Card Sound, the small bay between the Card Sound Bridge and the bank I had just passed through, was a quiet backwater. Today was no exception, and keeping to the eight-foot-deep water that lay about fifty yards from shore, I covered the perimeter of the bay without incident and headed out through the same pass in Card Bank that I had entered an hour earlier. It was a little on the short side for a patrol, but Martinez would know from my report that the bay was deserted.

The sun was on its way down as I cruised north. My next stop would be the Park Service dock and Susan's boat, but I didn't want to be that obvious if Martinez was watching me in real time on his computer, so I stayed toward the center of the bay. The chances of his watching were slim though, as I saw it was close to four. After his media victory yesterday, he would still be celebrating and either be finishing up his last hole or already be in the clubhouse.

As if I had just changed my mind, I cut the wheel to port and pushed the throttle forward. Twenty minutes later I entered the channel for the headquarters building. Slowly, I idled past Bayfront Park, not failing to notice the several boaters heading out for whatever activities the night offered avoided making eye contact with me. Leaving them on my port side, I took the small canal to the right and entered the Park Service docks.

It was close to five now and I hoped both Martinez and Susan had left for the day. Carefully I docked the center-console, using just the bow and stern lines to tie it off in the still water. With my phone in hand, I walked the ten feet to the finger pier leading to Susan's patrol boat, took a quick look around, and hopped on deck. I dropped to my knees, and with my phone already set to camera, I shot several pictures. After checking them quickly, I looked around and, seeing no one, got back aboard my boat. Several minutes later I was in the channel leading out to the bay.

I sat in front of my computer, wishing I was back on my island with a beer. Neither Martinez or Susan was around, so I figured it would be faster to use my office here. My phone lay in front of me and I typed the numbers in the bar code from the picture into the box on the computer screen. It appeared to accept the numbers and an hourglass started spinning, telling me it was working. Several seconds later the screen populated. Not surprisingly, there was much less data than my own log and it didn't take long to see Susan's daily routine.

I pulled out NOAA chart number 11463 from the rack in the hallway and returned to my desk. The chart showed the southern section of Biscayne Bay. Plotting the coordinates, I saw her pattern. Most of her trips were to the campgrounds on Elliott and Sands

Keys. There was one aberration. The day after I had found the body, there was a track from the headquarters dock to the lagoon. That was interesting. She was spying on me, either on her own or under orders from Martinez. In either case, it wasn't good, and I needed to find out the truth. To be thorough, I plotted the other data points from the computer screen and after finishing I was pretty sure they were all routine calls. Most were in areas of shallow water where boaters constantly grounded. It seemed that the only time Susan did her job was when there was a call and no one else was around to respond. Now that I had it, I had to decide what to do with the information.

I thought about Justine and the paint sample. Aside from the fact that I wanted to see her, there was pending evidence to review. I looked at my phone and saw it was seven. She would be at work. After sleeping until noon, my body was on a night schedule, and looking at the keys to the truck sitting on the desk next to me, I decided on a trip to town.

I caught a strange tone in Justine's voice when I called on my way to the lab. It didn't take me long to realize that once again I had put business above our personal relationship. I should have called her earlier, thanking her for last night. Scolding myself, I drove toward her office trying to figure out how to make it up to her.

STEVEN BECKER

A KURT HUNTER MYSTERY

BACKWATER BAY

"So, let me get this straight. You think Susan McLeash is doing illegal searches and spying on you?" Justine asked.

I was actually not sure what to think. "How else do you explain the GPS logs?" I asked, pushing the chart toward her.

We sat in a booth at a quiet Thai restaurant on South Dixie Highway. The staff sat across from us at a large round table eating their meal. It was close to nine o'clock, and on a weeknight, the only action once the clock struck double digits would be on South Beach.

"I can't figure out what Susan is doing. I ran her GPS logs and then found her aboard the Big Bang doing what I can only guess was an illegal search."

"If it were me, I'd be worried about who wants to blow the boat, and not your co-workers. Just sayin'."

I knew she was right. She had been around the politics and corruption of Miami-Dade for several years. My whining about Susan was getting zero traction. We sat in silence for a very long uncomfortable minute. Before my credit card even hit the table, the waiter scooped it up and ran the charge. We found ourselves ushered out and I couldn't help but hear the door lock behind us.

Standing in the parking lot, I looked at Justine and caught her eye. "Sorry, I tend to get carried away when I'm on a case." It wasn't much of an apology, especially since we'd already been through this. I hadn't listened to that voice in my head before. I only hoped it wasn't too late now.

"Hey, passion is good. How about we try and clear your head. I've got tomorrow off. It'd be cool to paddle around your place. The water there is beautiful."

I knew something was seriously wrong with me when I hesitated. Hoping she hadn't noticed, I agreed. "There's a kayak out on the island. I've had it out a few times. I'll try and keep up."

"You are on, my friend. Can we swing by my place?"

"You bet." My mind officially clocked out for the night. I drove Justine back to the crime lab, then followed her home. Being your typical male, I tried to wrestle the twelve-foot-six stand-up paddleboard by myself and cringed when it hit the ground. Justine stepped beside me, grabbed the handle, inverted the board, and easily lifted it onto the roof rack. With the board strapped to the rack and the paddle in the truck bed, I started the truck while she tossed her bag in the back and got in.

With the tip of her board visible in the windshield, I realized I had something new to be nervous about. Justine had already shown she was a better diver and boater than I was. Now I had to worry about her kicking my butt paddling. "How fast do you go on that thing?" My statement earlier about hoping to keep up was more of a prayer. She was an avid racer and one of the reasons she preferred the night shift was to practice. After hearing about her training regimen and how she had placed in some races, I was scared.

"Depends on the water and waves. If I'm pushing, I can hit six miles per hour. Maybe a little over if I can catch some waves."

I might be a California boy, but catching waves was not something I'd ever accomplished. I had learned enough about boats in the weeks I had been there to see that her board was lighter and longer than the old kayak I had been using. It would be faster.

"We can just tour around. No worries," she said, again seeming to read my mind.

"Sounds good," I said, not really thinking it.

Hauling her board around the back of the headquarters building, I was tempted to smile for the security cameras, thinking at the same time I had better be proactive and get a story ready. Surely, Martinez would spend the morning reviewing security footage—right after he checked my GPS log.

We stashed the board on the boat beside the center console and headed toward Adams Key. After a successful docking maneuver we were halfway up the walkway to the house, trying to make as little noise as possible. That mission failed, and I heard Zero bark before I saw him come bounding down the path. In any event, the security light picked up his near-round shape barreling toward us. He skidded to a stop and I saw a light come on at Becky and Ray's house. The screen door opened and a figure emerged.

"What the hell'd you do to Susie?" Ray asked.

I could see the outline of a smile on his face. "What do you mean?"

"Old McLeash was out here just a little bit ago looking for you. Girl had a bug up her butt bigger than usual." He spat. "And that's pretty goddamned big if you ask me."

I should have known she'd have some kind of alarm on her GPS tracking number. It was something I always wondered about with people: if they spent as much time working at work as they did being paranoid and watching their backs, they would probably be two promotions ahead. "Sorry about that. She didn't say what she wanted?"

"That's a tight-lipped broad on a good day. She just tied up, banged on your door, then stormed over to our house. Becky about bounced her ass back to the mainland until I got ahold of her. That Susan's one you don't want as an enemy. A good ol' *yes, ma'am, no, ma'am*, is what works for her type."

I had to agree with him and knew I had made a mistake. Turning back to the house to figure out damage control, I patted Zero on the head, said good night to Ray, and led Justine down the path. Zero followed us to the door and waited until Justine squatted down to pet him before he heeded Ray's screaming for him to come home.

Once inside, I opened two beers and handed Justine one. We sat next to each other on the couch in silence.

"Okay, she's a strange bird. Maybe you're not being paranoid," Justine admitted.

I nodded and hid behind the beer bottle, taking another sip instead of responding. I had already decided on the ride out to be very careful about making my relationship with Justine about work. "Want to go have a look at that old kayak I'll be chasing you in tomorrow?"

"Hmm," she said, sliding closer and taking the bottle from my hand.

When she leaned forward and kissed me, the work problem seemed to disappear.

———

I WAS SURPRISED WHEN I OPENED MY EYES. JUSTINE WAS BESIDE ME snoring quietly. Smiling, I looked toward the window and saw the first hint of daylight in the morning sky. It looked like a beautiful day. I rolled out of bed, trying not to wake her up. I thought I had succeeded when the roar of an outboard broke the silence. She woke with a start and our eyes met.

"Yeah, it's coming this way," I said, pulling on my shorts and T-shirt. "Hang for a minute and I'll see what's going on." Zero was released at the same time as I opened the door. Instead of running for me, he made a beeline for the dock, skidded to a stop, and started howling. I followed, hoping he had scared whoever it was away, but when I saw the tower and light bar on the boat being tied off to a cleat, I knew the dog would not deter the woman who stepped onto the dock.

She stood with her hands on her hips staring at me. Zero moved around her legs, sniffing at her. He stepped back and barked.

"Come here, boy, she won't bite," I said to Zero, thinking exactly the opposite, then turned to Susan. "Morning."

"Morning yourself. Aside from that board in your boat, what else have you been up to that you shouldn't be?"

I gave her the stupid-innocent look that guys have been giving women since the dawn of time. "Just doing my job."

"If your job involves tracking my movements, then I need to know about it."

Zero started pawing the ground like he wanted a piece of her. I used my leg to push him back, hoping Becky or Ray would help me out. I wondered why this tracking thing only went one way but thought that at least for now, I should leave it alone. "Don't you think we should be working the case instead of each other?" I tried to call her out nicely.

"We'll see what the boss has to say about this." She turned her back and stepped onto her boat.

The engine was still idling and a minute later, after slipping the dock lines, she turned to me. "Better watch yourself," she said, pushing the throttle down.

I felt Justine next to me. Ignoring her, I stared after the boat until it was just a small dot on the horizon.

"She's a pleasant one," Justine said.

I turned to look at her and forced a smile. "Yeah." There was not much to do except agree. Once she reported to Martinez, I was sure to get a call. The best thing I could do was to hit my scheduled route.

"If you need to work, I can go for a paddle and hang out. I don't want to get you in any trouble."

"No worries," I said, knowing I was probably in as much trouble as I could get in. "Let's do that paddle."

I hauled the kayak to the dock while she grabbed the paddleboard. We slid the boat into the water and I climbed down to the center-console to get in. There was an awkward moment when I tried to board, but I made it on—without the paddle. Slowly I started to drift away. Embarrassed for the second time in as many minutes, I used my hands to hold myself in place. "Haven't quite got this down yet."

Justine hopped into the center-console, slid her board into the water, and in less than a minute was by my side, handing over the paddle. Together we headed off to the small cut across Caesar Creek. Before we were even across the channel, she was two boat lengths ahead. I put my back into it, content to stay close and watch her from behind.

Once we were across, the mangroves blocked the wind and I gained on her. Together we slid past the area where Abbey had been found. Justine entered Jones Lagoon and I followed, wondering what she was up to. The first thing I noticed was the smell. Looking at the mangrove roots, I could tell it was the bottom of the tide. Nearly two feet of wet root was exposed.

As quickly as she had entered, Justine turned and exited the lagoon. "Smells nice in there!" she said, picking up the pace and leaving me behind.

"Hey, can we check out the spot where you caught the lobster? I've never been in there with the tide this low."

"Sure," she said.

I watched her lean over, adding additional power to her stroke.

Suddenly the board shot away and I lost her around a bend. I found myself at the entrance to the small lagoon, and knowing I would just get frustrated trying to keep up with Justine, I paddled easily into the estuary. Little fish jumped around me as I approached the far shore, where I had found the body.

Inspecting the mangrove roots as I paddled, I looked for anything I might not have seen earlier. A long white streak caught my eye. I imagined matching what looked like paint on the mangrove root to the gel coat on Susan's boat. My moment of glory ended when it turned out to be bird poop. I shook my head and was continuing my circuit of the lagoon when I heard an outboard motor approaching.

That in itself wasn't unusual, and I let it move into background noise before it suddenly dropped to an idle. A minute later, I could feel the wake push through the mangroves and rock the kayak. The boat must have been right on the other side of the mangroves. I moved closer, stashing the paddle when I hit the dense vegetation. Using my hands, I pulled the kayak in as far as it would go until I could just see the boat on the other side.

It was Susan's boat. She was talking into her phone and I heard my name.

22

BACKWATER BAY

"You know you have nothing on her, right?" Justine growled. "There could be a dozen reasons she was out there."

I was feeling bad enough cutting our paddle short and had been in such a rush to return that I had almost beaten her back to Adams Key. Her board had caught on the concrete dock, which cut a small gouge in the bottom when I tried to help her. We stood toe-to-toe staring at the scar. I felt the need to apologize, but the words were not coming out of my mouth. "And spying is on the top of the list." I was trying to control my anger without much success.

"Get real." She stalked toward the house.

"I'll fix it," I called after her, running my hand over the small gouge. I hoped with the few lessons in fiberglass repair I had gotten from Ray that I could actually pull it off—or I could buy him a twelve-pack and it would look as good as new.

"That's not the point. You're obsessed with Susan," she yelled back. The door slammed and she was gone.

I couldn't easily deny her claim. Instead, I did what men do when accused of something they're guilty of: I turned away and started working. Carefully I hosed off her board and took it to the house, where I placed it gently against the wall. I noticed how quiet it was and turned to Becky and Ray's house. Zero would have broken the tension perfectly. Their boat was gone and I guessed they had gone to the mainland.

Returning to the dock, I started to pull the kayak out of the water. It was still low tide and the water level was about five feet below the surface of the dock, making the task difficult. Struggling, I pulled up the line that was tied to the bow and lifted it. With the tide this low, the kayak hit the bottom of the concrete dock structure and stuck. Releasing the tension on the line, I dropped the kayak back in the water.

"Need some help?" Justine asked.

Surprised to see her, I took my hands off my hips and picked up the rope again, this time determined to lift the boat by myself. I got no further than I had on my first attempt. Without a word she came to my aid and together we were able to lift it out of the water. To my surprise, when the kayak reached the fulcrum point and was halfway onto the dock, I felt myself flailing in the air.

I landed in the water and looked up at Justine, wondering what had happened. It didn't take a special agent to see from the look on her face that she was still mad.

"Maybe you need to cool off and get some perspective," she said.

Before I could figure out what she was doing, she grabbed her board and in a move that defied gravity, hopped down to the center-console with it under her arm. Without looking at me, she released the lines. I was only feet away when the engine started and she pulled away from the dock. Seconds later, the boat was up on plane heading for the mainland.

Treading water, I watched until the tiny speck was gone, knowing I had blown it—again. I swam to the ladder and climbed onto the dock. The only boat left was the kayak. I reviewed my options: sit and wait until Becky and Ray got back, or take things into my own hands.

Fifteen minutes later, I had changed clothes and placed my gun and phone into a large Ziploc baggie. I walked back to the dock, hoping to see Becky and Ray coming to save me. Giving up on that, I stashed the baggie in one of the semi-watertight compartments, pushed the kayak back into the water, and maneuvered it to the ladder, where I was glad there were no spectators as I unceremoniously worked my butt into the cockpit.

Sitting this low, the mainland was barely visible. It was just a line on the water, so I decided to use the Turkey Point power plant's chimneys for navigation. Steering to the north of them, I started out. Fortunately, the wind was at my back, and although it made it hotter, the plastic shell was moving well.

Slowly I channeled my anger and started using my core. The kayak began to pick up speed and soon I was able to distinguish the landmarks of Bayfront Park. Adjusting course, I coasted to the dock, tired but proud. The feeling of accomplishing something faded fast when I saw Martinez standing over my boat and glaring at me.

"Suspending you wouldn't be out of the question."

I put my head down and hauled the kayak onto the dock. I didn't need him to point out the counts against me.

"It's a good thing that lady friend of yours works for Miami-Dade. I could probably fake the insurance if something happened. But what the hell are you doing? You're just adding to the list."

An electronic sound came from the kayak. I looked up at Martinez, who nodded, and I retrieved my phone from the compartment. The screen showed no caller ID. Any unknown caller would be better than the man standing in front of me so I answered.

"This Hunter?"

I recognized the voice. "Yeah."

"Johnny Wells here. You know that boat you asked me to keep a lookout for?"

"Yeah, the *Big Bang*." The volume was up and Martinez had moved closer, clearly able to hear and interested. As mad as he was, there was still some glory in it for him if I could solve the case. He mouthed for me to put the call on speaker.

"She pulled into a marina at Key Biscayne about an hour ago. Got word she's heading to the Bahamas in the morning."

I had mentioned to him the case I was working on, thinking they might make a run for it. "Thanks, man, what marina?"

"The one by Crandon Park."

I thanked him again and disconnected. Martinez backed away a few feet. He looked like he was analyzing what he thought he'd heard. I decided to explain. Watching his eyes, I could see the calculations in his head. After a long pause, he made his decision.

"Better check it out," he said, walking away as if nothing had happened. He was clearly staying on the side of the fence where he would get credit if things worked out and dodge responsibility if they didn't. I went to the center-console and saw the keys in the ignition. Silently thanking Justine for at least saving me that embarrassment, I untied the lines, hopped down to the deck, and started the engine. Popping into reverse a little too fast, I grazed the rub rail on a piling, but there was no way I was stopping to check it now.

Idling out of the channel, I worked the chart plotter with one eye and watched for boat traffic with the other. It was late afternoon and there was a steady stream of boats coming back into Bayfront Park. Thankfully, most gave the Park Service boat a wide berth. Whether it was my erratic steering or the light rail and logo, I didn't care.

I found the marina on the plotter, moved the cursor over it, and pressed the *GOTO* button. A solid red line appeared, and once I was past the last marker, I changed course and pushed down on the throttle. The marina was on the bay side of the island, and I followed the barrier islands until I was past Sands Key and the imaginary boundary of the park. Open water lay in front of me as I cruised toward the vague outline of land that the chart plotter said was Key Biscayne.

The wind had strengthened since my kayak run and now, running right into its teeth, I was taking spray with every third or fourth wave. The center-console was more of a bay boat, with a lower freeboard and little rise on the hull. I tried to adjust the speed and the trim, without much benefit. All I could do was duck down behind the console every time the bow slammed into a wave. With nothing to do except steer, my thoughts drifted to Justine, and with every wave that slammed against the hull, I hoped to pay a little penance for being an ass. I ran as hard as the boat was able. Staying dry was not important against the chance of losing the *Big Bang*. I chose the hard way, and despite my efforts, I arrived at the marina half an hour later soaked.

The marina was far smaller than I'd expected and I scanned the slips looking for the *Big Bang*. I couldn't spot her on my first pass and moved the boat closer for a better look. This time I cruised from pier to pier. The boat didn't magically appear. I idled over and docked by the fuel pumps near a building that looked like an office. Hogging both fuel hoses in front of me was the ICE Interceptor. I went to the boat and called out, but there was no answer. The attendant looked angry that the government was hogging his dock and pointed me in the direction of the office.

The air-conditioning hit me in the face when I entered. My wet uniform clung to my skin and in seconds, I was shivering. Johnny stood at the counter talking to a woman who was clearly uncomfortable with his uniform and questions. Seeing me only added to her discomfort.

"Hey, man. Thanks for the tip on the boat, but she's gone," I said. We moved out of earshot.

"We got some intel out of one of the boys on the shrimp boat that a load was coming ashore on the south end of the Key tonight. Pulled in for gas and saw her sitting here fueling up."

"Appreciate it. Any idea where she headed?"

"Pretty sure they hauled ass," the woman behind the counter had heard us anyway. "Word went out from the manager at the marina on South Beach that she had left port. He knew it was a crime scene and put a BOLO out on channel sixteen. Probably covering his butt for letting her slide out of there."

I said goodbye to Johnny and thanked the woman behind the counter. He followed me out the door.

"Got radar on that dinghy of yours?"

"Nope."

"We have a few hours before the rendezvous is scheduled to take place. I'm thinking the weather's a little snotty to be cruising around the Gulf Stream in that," he said, looking over at my boat, which was dwarfed by his cruiser.

"You think you can help me out?" I asked.

"Wouldn't have caught those smugglers if it weren't for you. We'll give it a few hours." He climbed aboard the cruiser. "I'll check the radar. Shouldn't be much action. In this kind of weather anyone out there is doing something they shouldn't be doing."

"Great. I'll see if I can get a slip for my boat and I'll be right over."

Heading back to the center-console, I stopped at the small shack by the fuel pumps. Johnny's boat had finished fueling and I knew I was low.

"Can I get a fill and a slip?" I asked the attendant.

He gave me a look that said he would be happy to get his dock back.

I hopped aboard and opened the gas cap with the two-pronged tool on the key chain. While the boat filled, I took my phone and gun from the console. I checked the screen and saw two messages from Justine. One had a smiley face, and the other asked me to call. I guessed she had either felt my pain on the paddle to the headquarters building and then the ride out here, or she had just cooled down.

The engines on the cruiser started and I saw Johnny look in my direction. My aching shoulders reminded me what Justine had done—she would have to wait. The autofill release went off with a loud click and I saw a splash of gas pop out of the tank. The attendant took the pump handle and handed me a paper towel to wipe the spilled gas off the hull. With a scowl he pointed at a slip across the way. I held a finger in the air, telling Johnny that I would just be a minute, and tossed the dock lines back to the attendant, catching a look that said he was happy to see me go. Probably Johnny too. I was pretty sure that government accounts didn't tip, and between the two of us, we were taking up the whole dock.

With the eyes of the ICE crew on me, I slid into the slip with only a light touch on one of the pilings. Satisfied, I tied off the boat and went to the Interceptor.

"I think we've got her on radar," Johnny said when I climbed aboard.

23

BACKWATER BAY

INCREDIBLE WAS the only word that came to mind as the Interceptor 39's deep V hull cut through the waves. The seaward side of the barrier islands was rougher than the protected passage I had taken, and yet the cockpit remained dry. I stood alongside Johnny, who was at the helm, steering with a light touch. To his right was another ICE agent working the electronics. The four three-hundred-horsepower engines hanging on the transom had the boat flying, skipping over the crests of the white-capped waves instead of smashing through them as my single two-hundred-fifty-horsepower engine did. After the beating I had just taken, this was luxurious.

"Contact five miles. Course one hundred eighty degrees," the agent yelled over the whine of the engines.

Johnny corrected course and added even more power now that the waves were at a forty-five-degree angle to the boat instead of coming straight at us. I glanced at the electronics and saw we were cruising at forty-eight knots. I guessed the boat could do sixty in calm seas. The radar screen showed several blips along the rings. We were fast approaching one of the smaller ones.

"That's probably her right there," Johnny said, and pointed to the blip. "Those bigger ones are tankers out in the Gulf Stream."

Just as he said it, I looked up and the *Big Bang* came into view. Although she was fast for a yacht, with a maximum speed of close to forty knots according to her specs, whoever was running her was being conservative. They seemed oblivious to our approach and within a few minutes, we were alongside.

Four faces stared to port and I guessed I had hit the jackpot. Brenda, Holly, and Herb were lined up against the gunwales looking at us. I could see Gordy at the helm above them. Brenda's eyes met mine and I could see the panic in her eyes.

There was every indication that she had the most to gain by taking the boat. She had been capable of hatching the plot but needed a co-conspirator. Gordy was the man for the job. I had done my homework and found there were no liens on the boat. The flyer at the brokerage office had a sales price of 1.8 million dollars. With the explosives and the insurance policy I suspected they had purchased for it, getting rid of the boat was a clear path to her divorce with a pot of gold at the end. If Gabe was blown up along with the boat, the rainbow would be brighter and the pot of gold bigger. There really was no worst-case scenario for her until Abbey figured out that the zincs were explosives. In my mind, I saw Abbey surface behind the boat and confront Brenda, who could easily have grabbed her air hose and hit the purge button on the regulator. With all the boat traffic in the marina, there was no telling who had run her over, but she was already dead when they did.

Now that body had been found, they were headed to the Bahamas. Their plan was likely to scuttle the boat there, under the assumption the Bahamian investigative process might be laxer, and if that failed they could battle the extradition process.

Someone yelling orders from the yacht brought me back to the present. I looked over at the bridge and the faces were gone. The boat was turning around, and I tried to figure out what they were up to. Before I could ask, Johnny picked up the microphone and flipped a switch on the cluttered dashboard.

"Vessel on our port side, heave to and go to channel nineteen, please." He set the microphone down and adjusted our speed and course to match the yacht's. "I don't know what game they're playing, but we need to end this. I have an appointment with some smugglers in an hour."

He said something to the other man, who reached into the console and came back with what looked like a pistol-grip assault rifle, but with a wider barrel. He loaded a canister into the chamber and nodded to Johnny. I knew how they were going to subdue them but not what the plan was after that.

The radio remained silent. The Interceptor continued to shadow the yacht. A minute later Johnny picked up the microphone again.

"Vessel on my port side. This is Immigration and Customs Enforcement. We are prepared to use force and board you if there is no response. Please go to channel nineteen."

The radio crackled. "This is the *Big Bang*. What can we do for you, sir?" It sounded like Gordy.

"Heave to and prepare to be boarded."

"Roger that, we were heading out and decided the weather was too bad to make a crossing. Can we handle this back at the dock?"

His plea fell on deaf ears. Johnny nodded to the agent beside him, who raised the tear gas gun and fired the canister. It landed with a clunk. A few seconds later, we could see the smoke drifting out of the open enclosure. The boat wallowed in the waves, coming beam to the seas, and all four aboard appeared on deck, coughing and wiping their eyes.

"She's all yours," Johnny said, easing the Interceptor alongside.

Two of the agents dropped fenders over the side and, using

grappling hooks, pulled the boats together. With both boats now beam to the seas, they rolled uncomfortably with each wave. The sound of fiberglass scraping together gave the situation a sense of urgency. Despite the fenders, the hulls met in each trough.

"You gotta go now," Johnny said with uncommon urgency. He was having a hard time working the throttles and wheels to keep the boats from damaging each other.

"Thanks," I called out as I moved to the gunwale. The boats were rocking badly enough that I had to wait for them to hit the crest of the same wave. When they were close to level, I hopped across. Landing on the deck, I found myself staring at four worried faces. I had no plan, but at least for the next few seconds, I had the threat of the Interceptor and ICE agents at my back. I pulled my gun just as the ICE agents released the boats. My focus stayed on the foursome, while they watched my backup pull away. I heard the whine of the engines and knew Johnny and his crew had left.

I was on my own now. Glancing at the faces in front of me, I saw the defeated looks. Whatever fight they'd had was gone—at least for now.

The boat wallowed in a trough, throwing me off balance. Recovering, I ordered Gordy back to the helm and the other three into the salon. My previous search had yielded no weapons, which made me a little more comfortable leaving them inside. Following Gordy up the ladder to the bridge, I took the seat next to him and watched as he increased power and pulled the boat back on course.

"Where are we headed?" he asked.

"Back to the marina," I said, holding the gun loosely on my thigh, wanting to keep the threat visible. It took him a minute to cross the cresting waves as he made the turn. We were out of sight of land, but glancing over at the chart plotter, I could see we were on course.

"What's going to happen to me?" Gordy asked.

I let that hang for a minute, trying to figure out how to use his position to my advantage. He was the only one not related to Abbey and might turn on the others. "Let's see how well you cooperate."

"Fair enough. You know it was all Brenda's plan."

Of course it was, except she was half-pickled most of the time and would have needed someone with some brainpower to handle the nuts and bolts. Herb and Holly, as accomplices, stood to make enough money to pay off their mortgage and have a fairly decent retirement. Gordy, as Brenda's confidant, and whatever else he was to her, was likely to gain a lot more.

I nodded, wanting to get him on my side at least until the *Big Bang* was back in her slip. Just in case he had any ideas, I watched him carefully and studied the controls. After I was confident I could tell if we were off course, I left him and went below to check on the others.

Their heads were close enough together that I could have cracked them like eggs. When the door opened they jerked away from each other. I had clearly interrupted some kind of planning session.

"We'll be back at the marina soon." Fisher Island was just coming into view on the port side. "Miami-Dade will meet us and sort this out then."

"But we haven't done anything," Herb said, moving closer to Holly.

I swear he almost said "yet." Holly was probably the most innocent one in the group. I looked at them again and noticed a bottle on the deck by Brenda's feet. She flinched when I moved toward her to lean over and pick it up. The last thing I needed was another case of the Brenda Braves. "Let's hold off on this until we clear this up."

I left them with the bottle in hand, draining what was left in a sink before I went back to the bridge. If it was full when she started I would have to keep an eye on her. When I reached the helm, we had just passed the point of South Beach and were in protected waters. The marina was around the bend now off our starboard side. Now that I had solved the problem of getting there, I had to figure out what to do when we were docked. Pulling out my phone, I called Miami-Dade to meet us.

I went with my gut and figured the first priority was getting the yacht safely to the dock. Gordy stayed on track and a few minutes later we were tied up. I ordered him down to the cabin and followed. It was time to sort this out.

STEVEN BECKER

A KURT HUNTER MYSTERY

BACKWATER
BAY

WE WERE in the salon staring at each other. Brenda and Holly sat close together. Gordy and Herb were as separate as the space allowed. I left them and stepped outside onto the deck to call Miami-Dade and see how long they'd be. As it turned out, the murder had happened in their jurisdiction. They would be making the arrest. They would also get the credit, and I wondered how that was going to go with Martinez.

Before I could make the call I heard a scream and with my gun drawn entered the salon. I had an instructor who had warned that desperate people were unpredictable. I had forgotten his advice, but Brenda reminded me when I saw the knife in her hand. I wasn't sure where she had been headed originally, but her fury turned to me. I stepped in front of her, ready to disarm her. The muscles in her neck tensed and I watched the knife come above her head. The brief pause at the top, just before she stepped forward to strike, was enough time for me to spin and grab her hand. It might have been the adrenaline or her rage, but her strength surprised me. I had to stop her before her arm passed below her head and she could put all her power behind the thrust.

A shadow passed behind me. I was so focused on Brenda that I didn't see Gabe until I felt the barrel of a gun in my back. I didn't know where he'd come from. Slowly, trying to stall, I dropped my gun at his command. The movement gave me a second to glance at Gabe, still standing behind me. His face was covered with blood. I turned back, off balance, and saw Brenda's arm come down out of the corner of my eye. In slow motion, I saw the arc of the knife and knew Gabe had no chance to escape.

Even though he held the gun, I knew it was only a threat. He had nothing to gain by a cold-blooded killing and I sensed he knew it. A life sentence would seriously interfere with his lifestyle. The tip of the knife was just inches away from his face when I pushed her. It was just enough to change the trajectory of the knife, which buried itself in the settee. Brenda, her hand still clutching the hilt, yanked hard, but the blade was stuck. She was bent forward in an awkward position. Wrapping both arms around her, I lifted her into the air and carried her across the room.

Before I released her, I felt her chest heave and knew she was broken. The fight had drained out of her and I set her gently on the floor. She curled her knees to her chest and I watched as tears streaked down her face.

"It was his fault," she sobbed. "I never meant to hurt her."

Brenda may have been disarmed and broken, but I was still looking into the barrel of the gun.

"All of you. Into the galley. Now," Gabe barked.

Herb and Holly moved quickly, picking Brenda up and taking her with them.

In a flash, I saw what I had missed. It was Gabe who had originally arranged for the explosives to be planted. Gordy had nothing to do with it except for setting up Abbey to clean the bottom and install the new zincs, which Gabe provided. His plan all along had been to pressure Brenda into running with the boat. When she did he would blow it up and take care of two problems at once, leaving Gordy the primary suspect. Gabe would have the insurance money and Brenda out of his hair. The plan had fallen apart when I discovered the case with the fake zincs in the stateroom. My haste to cover it up must have allowed Brenda to fine it and with Gordy's help figured out Gabe's plan. They had tried to turn the tables by abducting him, and it might have worked if not for my interference. By blowing the boat up in the Bahamas, they would collect on both the boat and Gabe's life insurance. Herb must have been checking that both policies were fully paid up when I followed him to the office the other day.

I took a chance and looked to see if Miami-Dade had arrived. When my head was turned, Gabe took me by surprise and rushed me. I tried to slide from his grasp but only managed to take him to the floor. He landed on top and when I opened my eyes I saw the gun pointed at my head. The muscles in his forearm tensed and I flinched, waiting for the shot, before I realized he was not going to shoot me here. We were too close to the marina to risk a gunshot. Instead, the stock of the gun made contact with my head.

I wasn't sure how long I had been out. Slowly I regained consciousness and opened my eyes. My vision was fuzzy, but I looked to be alone in the salon. I felt the vibration of the deck beneath me increase and feared the worst. Gabe was going through with his plan, and along with Brenda and company, I was going down with the ship.

The water, just fifteen minutes away outside of Government Cut, was open ocean. A mile offshore, he'd be in four hundred feet of water. At two miles it would be almost a thousand. Ditching the boat in water that deep would eliminate the possibility of a search.

My head ached where he had hit me and I tried to bring a hand to the wound to see if there was blood. I couldn't move and felt the hard plastic of a zip tie. My vision had cleared and I checked the cabin again. Alone, I worked my way to a sitting position. Shaking my head to clear the remaining cobwebs, I pulled my arms slowly apart, trying to work my wrists out of the bond. Twisting my arms until my hands were opposite each other in the restraints, I jerked as hard as I could. The plastic locking mechanism slipped but did not release.

Before I could try again, the boat lurched and stopped. I started to rise, but before I could gain my feet, I felt the bow slam a wave and was thrown off balance. I had a pretty good idea my theory was correct and we had headed out to sea. Thinking this would be the end, I tried the ties again. With my wrists together and scapulae retracted, I yanked my hands apart. I felt the tie split and I was free.

I was just about to rise when Gabe came back into the salon with the gun extended in front of him. I relaxed back into the position I had been in, feigning unconsciousness, and watched him through squinted eyes. He looked back at me as if suspecting something but stopped short when a voice hailed the boat.

"Special Agent Hunter, if you would take control of the vessel please."

For once, Susan McLeash's voice was welcome. It surprised Gabe, distracting him and giving me the seconds I needed to coil up and launch myself at him.

Our bodies met and we rolled around on the deck until the settee stopped our progress. Grunting like two high school wrestlers, we fought for the gun. We both froze for a second when a siren wailed and Susan hailed the boat again.

The distraction worked in my favor and I pulled the gun from his grasp. He still had some fight left, which I quickly dispatched in the same manner he had used to knock me out. A minute later, he was cuffed to one of the table legs that was bolted to the floor. I wanted some answers from him, but the voice hailing the boat made me cringe.

After checking Gabe to make sure he was secure, I opened the door. Squinting for real in the bright sun, I looked forward and saw Susan McLeash in her Park Service boat sitting perpendicular to the path of the yacht. With her back to the helm, she leaned against the leaning post.

I nodded and, keeping my head down, went back inside. About to go up the short flight of stairs to the bridge, I paused and backtracked to the galley. Herb, Holly, and Brenda were still there, their hands zip-tied behind their backs and sitting on the floor. Brenda growled at me. The others sat silently, resigned to their fate.

Gordy was still at the helm. I restrained him with a real zip tie from my belt, leaned out the side door, and held up my phone. Susan acknowledged that calling would be more discreet than yelling across the decks or using the open line of the VHF.

"Appreciate the help," I said, trying to initiate a truce when she answered.

"Let's get this vessel back to the dock," was all she said.

I looked around and saw that this had all taken place within sight of the dock. The wave I had felt must have been Susan's boat wake.

I nodded and disconnected, knowing I would need all my newly-learned skills to dock the boat. Three times longer and twice as wide as my center-console, she was intimidating. Fortunately, she was a single engine, or I would have really embarrassed myself. Using the throttle, I backed and cut the wheel hard to port until the momentum of the boat had it parallel with Susan's. Then, slowly, I nudged the throttle forward. The boat reacted nicely and I steered toward the marina. Glancing back, I saw Susan following at a safe distance.

Unsure of her part in all this, I warily decided to take her help at face value. It was totally consistent with her MO to arrive like the cavalry to bail me out and push any guilt away from her. Putting that aside, I focused on getting the boat back into the slip.

We had just entered the marina and I dropped a few hundred RPMs, trying to go as slow as I could without losing steerage. The water was calm and the boat moving slow enough that I felt motion below me. Over the low rumble of the engine, I heard a shot, then another.

Before I could react I felt a barrel in the small of my back for the second time today.

"Go ahead and dock it. Then we're walking off together," Brenda said.

I wasn't sure how she had gotten out of the zip tie or where the gun had come from. Then I realized it was mine. I tried to ignore her. An idea started to form. If she wanted the boat docked, I would do just that. It would take all my concentration to get the boat into the tight quarters of the slip without damaging it or one of the other multimillion-dollar boats docked adjacent to it. Susan still hovered just outside the turning basin. She was far enough away that I didn't think she'd heard the shots or could see Brenda behind me. There was nothing I could do except finish docking the boat.

For my plan to work, I needed to back in. Running the boat forward as far as I could, I jammed the transmission into reverse to stop just before I would hit the gleaming catamaran across the narrow channel from the slip. The boat stopped and I turned, placing my butt against the wheel. I found myself looking down the gun sight backward at Brenda. I could clearly see her pupils were dilated in her wide-open eyes. She was still in shock, and that made reasoning with her a long shot. My hand remained on the throttle, and I pulled back slightly. When I heard the transmission click, I yanked hard and went for her.

The boat slammed against the dock, throwing both of us off balance. I was expecting it and she wasn't, but it didn't matter when a loud boom shook me. Not knowing whether I was shot or not, I continued pressing forward until I had the warm barrel in my grasp. I pulled hard and it came free—almost too easily. Brenda's body fell to the deck and tumbled over Gordy who was secured to one of the stainless steel rails. A pool of blood started to spread out from her head.

I held the gun and stared at her. Something nudged the bow of the boat and I looked up to see Susan's boat pressed against the yacht. She was standing by the leaning post of the center-console with a rifle in her hand.

BACKWATER BAY

KNOWING that Susan had probably saved my life didn't help anything. I had to regroup and get my wits about me before I had to explain myself or what happened. Fortunately, the gunshots bought me some time. I brought Gordy, now covered in Brenda's blood, down to the galley, where Herb and Holly were still bound, with confused looks on their faces. I left them there for the time being as this would likely be the extent of their incarceration. I didn't think either of them had committed an actual crime. Before I left, I saw blood on the range. A desperate Brenda must have used a metal edge to maul her zip tie and escape, cutting herself in the process. I moved through the salon. Gabe was still handcuffed to the table leg, but he was on the floor, with a pool of blood around him. Walking past him, I opened the salon door and was confronted by a handful of Miami-Dade officers with their guns trained on me. Finally, the cavalry had arrived. With my hands in the air, I explained who I was and slowly reached for my credentials.

They came aboard. In minutes the boat was crawling with officers and soon after that with crime scene investigators. After walking the first group of detectives through the crime scene and giving the short version of what happened, I looked toward the bow, but Susan was gone.

The adrenaline I had been living on for the past few days was spent and I sat on the transom with a bottle of water watching the crime scene folks do their work. I would have preferred a drink, but with gunshots fired and two people dead, I figured I would have to give a statement. There were the usual yellow cards with numbers scattered across the deck. Herb, Holly, and Gordy had been taken into custody. Gabe and Brenda's bodies remained where they had fallen, waiting for the medical examiner to arrive. Until then the camera ran nonstop, taking pictures of the bodies and deck from every vantage possible.

"I can't believe there are dead bodies here and you didn't call me."

I looked up to see Justine hovering over me. Behind her was Vance, the chief medical examiner, who nodded and went to the salon. "Things got a little out of hand."

"I'll say. That other agent, Susan, shot Brenda?"

"And Brenda shot Gabe. How convenient."

I wondered how she knew about Susan, then followed her look and saw Susan's boat tied off to the starboard rail. She was aboard talking to the two detectives I had seen in the crime lab. I tried not to smile.

"Yeah. I'm still not sure what her agenda is."

"Maybe you should ask her," Justine said.

I looked back at the Park Service boat. The detectives were exchanging cards and shaking hands with her. I got up and crossed to the other side of the boat. "Can we talk?" I asked her.

"Sure. Come on aboard," Susan answered.

Justine had already started to work with Vance and I felt a pang of jealousy watching her laugh at something he said. Shaking that off, I climbed over the rail and stepped onto the twin of my boat—only this one was spotless. I'd have bet I wouldn't find a fishing rod aboard.

"I guess I should thank you for taking out Brenda." I was very careful not to say that she had saved my life. The last thing I needed was to acknowledge a favor like that with Susan McLeash.

"I saw the gun come up."

She said it like there was nothing else she could have done. There wasn't any remorse in her tone; she was just matter-of-fact. "Well anyway, I appreciate the backup." I paused before I asked, "How did you come to be here?" I thought I knew the answer already.

"Somebody has to keep an eye on you. Martinez wanted you on a short leash."

"I hope I didn't disappoint," I said. She had confirmed what I expected. The GPS log still bothered me, but how far do you push someone who just saved your life?

She gave me a look that I remember my mother giving me. Kind of a cross between angry and disappointed. "If you would have been a little more open, there might not be blood all over your uniform."

I looked down at my shirt and saw the blood splatter. Acknowledging her, I nodded. "Guess I owe you one."

THE CRIME SCENE WAS PRETTY MUCH CLEANED UP. IT HAD TAKEN A while. After the case containing the explosives was found rigged to a detonator, the bomb squad had to be called in. I had just finished giving my statement to the Miami-Dade officers.

Susan had given her statement before I had and left, taking the answers to some of my questions with her. There were still some loose ends that didn't make sense, like why she was even there in a position to help me. I wasn't sure how the dust would settle and if Martinez or the Park Service would get any credit by the time

Miami-Dade was done. I'd just have to wait and figure it was going to be business as usual tomorrow.

"You want to go talk or something?" Justine asked. "I'm wrapped up here."

I looked back at the deck and saw Brenda's body being taken away on a gurney. Gabe's body was already loaded in the coroner's van and the crowd aboard the *Big Bang* was thinning out. "Sure, that'd be good." I looked down at my bloodstained shirt and shrugged. "I'm kind of a mess and have no transportation." I hadn't told her how I had gotten there.

"The story of your life. Come on, we can go to my place. I'll cook something for us."

There was nothing left for me there and I followed her to her car. We drove in silence to her condo and after a long hot shower, I found her in the kitchen working on a stir-fry.

"Looks really good," I said, moving behind her and kissing her neck. Thankfully she didn't flinch, but rather eased her body into mine. We hadn't really talked since she had taken the boat.

"There's a bottle of wine on the counter. How about you open it and pour us a glass."

I followed orders and a few minutes later we were sitting at her counter with plates piled high and large glasses of wine. I ate slowly, savoring the ginger and garlic Justine had used to flavor the dish. The wine went down easily and our plates were soon empty.

"I'll get the dishes," I said, standing up and taking both plates to the kitchen.

"Forget that, but bring the wine back with you."

She was on the couch when I returned. Topping off both glasses, I sat next to her. There was a reluctant peace falling over me, as if I were finally relaxing. But there were a few questions still bothering me: how did Susan know to show up at the marina and who actually killed Abbey? Justine must have sensed my turmoil.

"It's hard when they don't wrap up cleanly."

I brought the wineglass to my lips and took a long sip. It wasn't for the drink, but rather to keep my mouth shut. I knew the best thing I could do was to let it go. The three remaining conspirators were all in custody. If they managed to evade prison, they were broke with no prospects. They would each pay in their own way for their part in this. I didn't know what charges would have been hanging over Gabe and Brenda if they were still alive and guessed it didn't really matter anymore. I had set out to get justice for Abbey, and in the end, I had succeeded.

As for Susan, I had no idea if she was under orders from Martinez or working on her own to undermine my success and take some credit herself. I decided not to dwell on that. If I judged my successes and failures by commendations, I was in this for the wrong reasons. If she had stepped over the line this time, maybe I couldn't prove it, but I was sure there would be a next time, and I would be watching for it.

I took a last sip and set the glass on the table. Justine did the same and we fell into each other's arms. As I leaned in to kiss her, I realized that maybe I had finally learned to separate business from pleasure.

BACKWATER CHANNEL

Get the next book in the Kurt Hunter Mystery Series now:
You'd think a nuclear power plant was dangerous enough ...

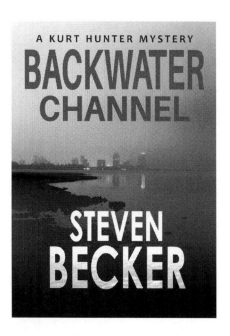

That's what special agent Kurt Hunter thought until, while out fishing, he witnesses a murder at the Turkey Point nuclear power plant. After being assigned the case, Kurt is pulled into the convoluted politics of Miami only to find out that the embattled power plant is only a pawn in a more deadly game.

Greed and corruption are nothing new to pristine Biscayne Bay. With the plants miles of cooling canals providing essential habitat for several endangered species, Kurt is thrown into a rift between waring environmentalists and power hungry corporate executives all trying to advance their own agendas.

Get it now!

ABOUT THE AUTHOR

Always looking for a new location or adventure to write about, Steven Becker can usually be found on or near the water. He splits his time between Tampa and the Florida Keys - paddling, sailing, diving, fishing or exploring.

Find out more by visiting www.stevenbeckerauthor.com or contact me directly at booksbybecker@gmail.com.

facebook.com/stevenbecker.books
instagram.com/stevenbeckerauthor

Get my starter library First Bite for Free!
when you sign up for my newsletter

http://eepurl.com/-obDj

First Bite contains the first book in several of Steven Becker's series:

Get them now (http://eepurl.com/-obDj)

Mac Travis Adventures: The Wood's Series

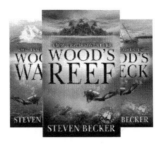

It's easy to become invisible in the Florida Keys. Mac Travis is laying low: Fishing, Diving and doing enough salvage work to pay his bills. Staying under the radar is another matter altogether. An action-packed thriller series featuring plenty of boating, SCUBA diving, fishing and flavored with a generous dose of Conch Republic counterculture.

Check Out The Series Here

★ ★ ★ ★ ★ *Becker is one of those, unfortunately too rare, writers who very obviously knows and can make you feel, even smell, the places he writes about. If you love the Keys, or if you just want to escape there for a few enjoyable hours, get any of the Mac Travis books - and a strong drink*

★ ★ ★ ★ ★ *This is a terrific series with outstanding details of Florida, especially the Keys. I can imagine myself riding alone with Mac through every turn. Whether it's out on a boat or on an island....I'm there*

Kurt Hunter Mysteries: The Backwater Series

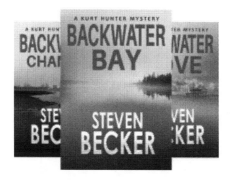

Biscayne Bay is a pristine wildness on top of the Florida Keys. It is also a stones throw from Miami and an area notorious for smuggling. If there's nefarious activity in the park, special agent Kurt Hunter is sure to stumble across it as he patrols the backwaters of Miami.

Check it out the series here

★★★★★ *This series is one of my favorites. Steven Becker is a genius when it comes to weaving a plot and local color with great characters. It's like dessert, I eat it first*

★★★★★ *Great latest and greatest in the series or as a stand alone. I don't want to give up the plot. The characters are more "fleshed out" and have become "real." A truly believable story in and about Florida and Floridians.*

Tides of Fortune

What do you do when you're labeled a pirate in the nineteenth century Caribbean

Follow the adventures of young Captain Van Doren as he and his crew try to avoid the hangman's noose. With their uniques mix of skills, Nick and company roam the waters of the Caribbean looking for a safe haven to spend their wealth. But, the call "Sail on the horizon" often changes the best laid plans.

Check out the series here

★★★★★ *This is a great book for those who like me enjoy "factional" books. This is a book that has characters that actually existed and took place in a real place(s). So even though it isn't a true story, it certainly could be. Steven Becker is a terrific writer and it certainly shows in this book of action of piracy, treasure hunting,ship racing etc*

The Storm Series

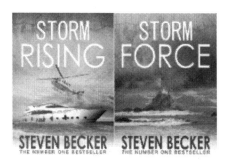

Meet contract agents John and Mako Storm. The father and son duo are as incompatible as water and oil, but necessity often forces them to work together. This thriller series has plenty of international locations, action, and adventure.

Check out the series here

★★★★★ *Steven Becker's best book written to date. Great plot and very believable characters. The action is non-stop and the book is hard to put down. Enough plot twists exist for an exciting read. I highly recommend this great action thriller.*

★★★★★ *A thriller of mega proportions! Plenty of action on the high seas and in the Caribbean islands. The characters ran from high tech to divers to agents in the field. If you are looking for an adrenalin rush by all means get Steven Beckers new E Book*

The Will Service Series

If you can build it, sail it, dive it, and fish it—what's left. Will Service: carpenter, sailor, and fishing guide can do all that. But trouble seems to find him and it takes all his skill and more to extricate himself from it.

Check out the series here

★★★★★ *I am a sucker for anything that reminds me of the great John D. MacDonald and Travis McGee. I really enjoyed this book. I hope the new Will Service adventure is out soon, and I hope Will is living on a boat. It sounds as if he will be. I am now an official Will Service fan. Now, Steven Becker needs to ignore everything else and get to work on the next Will Service novel*

★★★★★ *If you like Cussler you will like Becker! A great read and an action packed thrill ride through the Florida Keys!*